D1415298

THE BOBBSEY TWINS'
TOY SHOP

THE BOBBSEY TWINS BOOKS
By Laura Lee Hope

"Oh, look what I found in Chi Chi's pocket!"
Flossie exclaimed.

The Bobbsey Twins' Toy Shop

The Bobbsey Twins' Toy Shop

By

LAURA LEE HOPE

GROSSET & DUNLAP
Publishers   New York

COPYRIGHT, 1948, BY
GROSSET & DUNLAP, INC.
ALL RIGHTS RESERVED

———————

PRINTED IN THE UNITED STATES OF AMERICA

CONTENTS

THE BOBBSEY TWINS'
TOY SHOP

CHAPTER I

THE MYSTERY SHIP

BERT BOBBSEY jumped the back fence and ran to the house. He had a baseball catcher's mask in his hand.

"What's the matter, Freddie?" he asked, stopping to see what his younger brother was doing.

At the porch step Freddie was working with a hammer and screw driver on a toy fire engine. His twin sister Flossie stood looking on.

"This engine's broken," Freddie answered. "It's one of my best engines, too. It has a whistle, but it won't whistle."

Bert looked at the engine. The whistling sound was made by a small air pump.

"The connection's broken," he said. "You'd better let Uncle Linn fix it."

Uncle Linn was not a real uncle to the Bobbsey twins. He was a kind, elderly man who lived a few blocks away, and was an expert at mending toys.

1

"He can fix just about anything," said Flossie. "Freddie, why don't you take your engine to him?"

"Guess I will," her twin answered.

"I'll go along," said Bert. "Some wires on this catcher's mask are loose. I'll bet Uncle Linn could put 'em in place."

"Oh, I want to go, too," said Flossie quickly. "One of my dolls swallowed her eyes, and I want Uncle Linn to get 'em back again."

"What do you mean, your doll swallowed her eyes?" Freddie scoffed.

"There's nothing but holes where Marie's eyes ought to be," said Flossie. Marie was one of her favorite dolls.

"Probably they fell back inside her head," was Bert's opinion. "Well, bring her along." Then he added, "Where's Nan?"

Nan was Bert's twin sister. They were a few years older than Flossie and Freddie, who were six. The younger twins had blonde hair and blue eyes like their mother. Nan and Bert were dark like Mr. Bobbsey.

"Nan's upstairs," said Flossie. "Why'd you want to know?"

"Because we're going to play tennis."

"Nan can't play," Flossie giggled. "Her tennis

racket broke. Everything around here's getting broken."

"We'd better all go to Uncle Linn's," Freddie suggested.

Bert said he thought fixing a tennis racket was a special kind of job. He was not sure a toy mender could do it. The boy called to his twin, and she came downstairs. Nan agreed with Bert about the racket, but said:

"I'll go with you to Uncle Linn's. I love his toy-mending shop."

Nan and Bert walked together down the street. Flossie and Freddie followed. A few minutes later they reached the main street of Lakeport. As the children passed the secondhand shop of Jacob Lenter, Bert pointed to the show window.

"Look at that!" he exclaimed. "Gee, that's swell!"

"You mean that doll?" asked Flossie, her big blue eyes lighting up as she wished the lovely, antique doll were hers. It looked very beautiful standing there.

"No," Bert answered. "I mean that model of a ship. It's a schooner, and all rigged, too. I'd like to own that!"

"Would you?" a voice asked unexpectedly.

The children looked up and saw plump, jolly

Mr. Lenter standing in the doorway. He smiled at them.

"What ship is this a model of, Mr. Lenter?" Bert inquired.

"It's a model of a mystery ship that sank years ago in the river off Stony Island," answered Mr. Lenter.

"A mystery ship?" asked Nan.

"Yes," replied the secondhand-shop owner. "The ship was the schooner *Spray*. She went down in a storm. There was an explosion, I believe."

The twins knew Stony Island. They had been there on picnics many times. But they had never heard about the wreck.

"I'd sure like to have that model," said Bert, gazing at it admiringly. "Does it cost much?"

"I'll let you have it for two dollars, Bert," answered Mr. Lenter, who knew the Bobbsey twins well. "I paid that for it to a sailor; the only man saved when the *Spray* sank. The model's been knocking around my shop a long time, just gathering dust. Some boy named Danny said he was going to buy the ship, but he never came back to get it. I'll be glad to sell it to you, Bert."

"I'll buy it," was the quick answer. "But I

haven't any money with me. I'll have to pick it up later."

"I'll trust you for the money," the second-hand dealer said.

"Thanks, but I can't take the ship now," Bert replied. "I'll call for it later on."

"After we get my engine fixed," said Freddie.

"And my doll that swallowed her eyes," added Flossie.

Mr. Lenter laughed. Then he said, "I'll bet you're going to Uncle Linn Smith's." The children nodded. "Well, the model will be here for you when you come back, Bert. I'm not going to wait any longer for that boy Danny."

"What was the mystery about the real ship that sank?" Nan asked.

"Oh, something about a missing treasure— money, or something valuable supposed to be on board," Mr. Lenter replied.

"I found a treasure once!" exclaimed Freddie. "It was a big silver dollar."

"Once," chimed in Flossie, "I found a four-leaf clover. That's supposed to bring good luck, but right after that Marie swallowed her eyes."

The Bobbsey twins continued on down the street. Bert remarked to Nan:

"That ship model will look swell up in my room."

"*Our* room," Freddie corrected his brother, because he and Bert occupied the same bedroom. "I can look at the ship, too, and sail it in the bathtub."

"Don't you dare touch that model," Bert warned him. "It's not a toy, and probably wouldn't float."

"A ship model's just for decoration," Nan explained to her younger brother.

"Huh," said Freddie in disgust, no longer interested in the model.

"If there's a treasure in that sunken ship in our river, why hasn't some diver gone down and located the gold on it?" Bert wondered aloud.

"Mr. Lenter didn't say it was gold," said Nan, as she stopped Flossie and Freddie from crossing a street against the red light.

"Well, whatever it was, you'd think divers would have found it," Bert insisted. "It sure is a mystery."

Soon after this the twins turned into the street on which Uncle Linn's toy shop was located. The shop was in a big, old-fashioned barn back of the Smith house.

Uncle Linn had retired from business. After

his wife died, he made a hobby of mending broken toys. Next door to him lived his sister, Mrs. Pry, called Aunt Sallie by the children. Her husband had died, so she and her brother lived more or less together, though in separate houses. Aunt Sallie did the housework and the cooking. Uncle Linn took care of all their business affairs, because his sister was very deaf.

As the Bobbsey twins turned into the driveway between the two houses and headed for the old barn, Aunt Sallie came out of her house and greeted them.

"Hello," said Bert. "Where's Uncle Linn?"

"Oh, dear me!" exclaimed Aunt Sallie. "That's too bad. Who'd you say hurt your shin?"

"I didn't say *'shin,'* I said 'Linn,' Aunt Sallie," Bert said, somewhat louder.

"The best thing for a bruised shin," the old lady went on, "is a plaster of burdock leaves."

Freddie and Flossie began to giggle.

"Sh!" said Nan, knowing that, because of her deafness, Aunt Sallie had not understood.

Freddie and Flossie remembered their manners and stopped laughing. Bert finally made the elderly lady understand he wanted to see her brother. She laughed now herself, saying she ought to wear her hearing aid all the time.

"I might have guessed from the toys you're carrying that you want them mended," she said. "You'll find Linn in his workshop."

The twins hurried to the big barn. It was a quaint, curious place. The horse stalls had been taken out, and the place filled with benches, tables, and shelves. On them lay a clutter of broken toys, half-mended toys, and others ready to be delivered to new owners. A large part of Uncle Linn's work was collecting and mending toys to be given to children who had few toys of their own.

The tools the toy mender used were lying about, with pots of glue and paste scattered among them. There was also a pile of small boards used in making repairs.

Altogether, the workshop, while rather untidy, had an air of good cheer and happiness about it. Even the damaged clown dolls, of which there were several, had not lost their wide, comical grins.

In the midst of it all sat Uncle Linn. The white-haired man always seemed to be smiling as he worked, and he had an amusing habit of making up funny little verses on the spur of the moment. As he invited his callers to step inside, he said:

"Come in! Come in!
To your Uncle Linn,
But take care where you walk,
Or my donkey may balk."

The twins looked around. Near the door stood a small wooden donkey, his hind feet kicking into the air. Flossie pretended to be afraid, and jumped aside. The others laughed.

"What's the trouble with your doll, Flossie?" asked Uncle Linn, as if he were a nice doctor inquiring about a child patient. "Is she running a fever?"

"No. It's her eyes," Flossie said. "She used to open and close 'em, but she can't any more."

"I'll mend her," promised the kindly toy maker. "And what's your trouble, Freddie? I'll bet your fire engine can't whistle any more."

Freddie stared. "How—how'd you know?" he gasped.

Uncle Linn laughed. "You have your finger right on the whistle button, but it's not making a sound."

"You know just everything," said Nan, smiling. Then, looking around, she added, "You have an awful lot of work. How are you ever going to finish it?"

"Oh, the work will go fast enough." The toy mender smiled. "It's all in knowing how to find the trouble spots in the broken toys. Well, I'll fix your toys in a few days. Lay them over there, will you?"

The Bobbseys put the doll, the fire engine, and the catcher's mask on a bench, then looked around at the many other toys to be mended. Freddie spied a fire engine in much worse condition than his. He decided at once that he would give his whistling fire engine to some child who did not have one. When he told this to Flossie, she said a bit reluctantly:

"Maybe I'll give Marie away. I—I love her a lot, though."

Presently Bert said, "Come on. I want to get that ship model before Danny Rugg decides to buy it after all."

"Was it Danny Rugg who wanted the model?" asked Nan in surprise.

"I don't really know," said Bert. "But I'm afraid it might be."

Danny Rugg was a boy Bert's age whom none of the Bobbseys liked. He was quarrelsome, and always making trouble.

"If it *is* Danny Rugg, and he finds out I've bought the model of the *Spray,* he'll sure be sore," Bert declared, after the children left the shop.

"Don't tell him," advised Flossie, running alongside the older twins.

"He—he might fight you," declared Freddie.

Just as the children reached the street, they heard a crash in the toy shop. It was followed by a groan and a voice calling:

"Help! Help!"

"That's Uncle Linn!" exclaimed Nan.

"He must be hurt!" cried Bert, starting to run back. "Come on!"

CHAPTER II

A CLOWN DOG

AS THE Bobbsey twins ran toward the old barn, Uncle Linn cried out again:

"Help! Help! Somebody come and lift this bench off me!"

When Bert and Nan entered the barn, they saw the old toy mender lying on the floor, a heavy workbench upside down across his chest and arms. They tugged at it for several seconds before they were able to lift the bench off. Then, as Nan took the old man's arm to help him up, he cried out in pain.

"Seems like my right arm's broken," Uncle Linn wailed.

"Oh, dear!" Nan exclaimed. "Freddie, Flossie, get Aunt Sallie!"

As the small twins ran off, she and Bert gently raised Uncle Linn to his feet and got a chair for him. He was very pale.

"I'll get you a drink of water," Nan offered, seeing a sink in one corner of the toy shop.

"This is bad—very bad," murmured Uncle Linn, as he looked at his useless right hand. "I won't be able to keep on with my work. Oh, dear! This is terrible!"

"Drink this," urged Nan, offering him the glass of water.

Then, like the nurse she hoped to be some day, Nan made a sling from a strip of cloth lying on a bench. She adjusted it around Uncle Linn's neck, passing it gently under his arm between his wrist and elbow the way she had been taught in a first-aid class at school. Next Nan tied a knot in the sling, so the injured arm and hand could rest against Mr. Smith's chest.

"That's better. That's fine, Nan," he murmured, leaning back in the chair. "But I don't see how I can keep on with my toy-repair work. There's mending to be done, and painting, and gluing— And now I can't do it. Oh, why did this have to happen?"

"Maybe," suggested Nan eagerly, "we could help you in your toy shop."

"Oh, do you think you could?" the injured man asked.

It was characteristic of the Bobbsey twins that they were always ready and willing when anyone needed help. Recently a man who ran a traveling amusement park had asked them to get him something, for which they had searched far and wide, and which they finally found in Mexico!

This was only one of many places to which the twins had traveled, and one of many adventures they had had. At this moment it looked as if a new adventure might be starting right here in Lakeport!

Before Uncle Linn could say anything more about the Bobbseys helping him in the toy shop, Aunt Sallie came hurrying into the barn. Giving one look at her brother, she said:

"Bert, go call Dr. Benson."

Bert ran to the telephone in the house. The physician, whose office was not far away, promised to come over at once. Nan thought the Bobbseys should leave, but Uncle Linn insisted that they stay.

"Children always make me feel better," he declared. "If you twins leave, I know my arm's going to feel worse. Anyhow, if the doctor says I can't use my hand, Bert and Nan will have to run this shop."

"Really!" exclaimed Aunt Sallie, who had on her hearing aid now and could hear very well.

Uncle Linn refused to say anything more about

his idea until after the physician's call. Dr. Benson arrived in a few minutes.

"Well, well," he said, "someone's made a very fine sling to hold your arm, Mr. Smith. Did Mrs. Pry do that?"

"No, my sister Nan did," spoke up Flossie proudly.

"Hm," said the doctor, as he examined the injured toy mender. "If Nan's that handy, maybe she can help you some more. Mr. Smith, your wrist is broken, and you won't be able to use your right hand for a long time!"

"Oh, dear!" said Aunt Sallie.

"That's what I was afraid of," declared Uncle Linn sadly. "And so much work to be done here."

"Now don't you go fretting and stewing about the toy shop," said Aunt Sallie. "Let the work go!"

"Oh, no, I couldn't do that," her brother declared. "With Christmas only a few months off, and times sort of hard for some people, lots of children will be needing new toys."

"But you'll have to give it up now," protested Aunt Sallie.

"Oh, but I mustn't!" he insisted. Then, with a searching look at Bert and Nan, he said, "Do you children think if I tell you what to do, you could help me in the toy shop?"

"We can try," the twins said together, their eyes dancing excitedly. Nan added, looking around, "We could start on the easy jobs."

"Sure," declared Bert.

Aunt Sallie said that Mr. and Mrs. Bobbsey would have to give their permission.

"Come back tomorrow with your answer," she told the twins.

The children hurried off eagerly. Freddie and Flossie insisted that they were going to help too, but Nan and Bert warned them not to try anything unless Uncle Linn told them it was all right.

Upon arriving home, the twins learned from Dinah, the Negro cook, that their mother had gone out.

"She'll likely get home when yo' daddy does," the stout woman said, smiling.

Disappointed not to get their answer at once about working in the toy shop, Nan, Flossie, and Freddie decided to stay at home and wait for Mrs. Bobbsey. Bert took some money out of his bank and started down to Mr. Lenter's for the ship model.

"Yo' all stay outdoors an' play," Dinah directed Flossie and Freddie. "But don't get yo'-selves in no mischief. I got washin' to do, an' I don't want to be upset by somethin' happenin'!"

"I know what let's do," said Flossie, her blue eyes sparkling.

"What?" asked Freddie.

"Let's dress Waggo up like a clown and make him do tricks."

"Sure! That'll be fun!" agreed Freddie.

Waggo, the fox terrier, was a lively little dog. He was a great worry to the Bobbseys' older dog Snap, who, because he was so old, had lost his former playful ways. Waggo was always ready to romp with the twins. But Snap preferred to lie in his kennel in the sun, and sleep.

Flossie had turned one of her dolls' dresses and a hat into a clown suit. After a lot of coaching she and Freddie had taught Waggo to prance around in it on his hind legs. Calling the little terrier from where he was trying to make Snap come out and play, they put the clown suit on him.

"Now walk like a circus clown," Flossie ordered. "Walk, Waggo! Walk!"

Freddie straightened the cap on Waggo's head. The terrier stood on his hind legs and pranced about the yard. Presently Dinah came from the laundry with a basket of clothes she had just washed.

"Waggo sho' looks cute," she remarked. "Just like a wound-up toy."

While Dinah was pinning several towels on the line, Freddie and Flossie tried teaching Waggo some new tricks. They rolled a little barrel from the garage and put the terrier on it. Freddie pushed the barrel gently, and Waggo was supposed to make his little legs go very fast, so he could stay on. But he kept jumping off instead.

"I guess we'll just have to let him walk on the ground," sighed Flossie. "Walk, Waggo!" she commanded.

The little terrier stood up again, but almost at once he dropped back on all fours, and with an angry bark leaped toward the back fence.

"Somebody must be coming, and Waggo doesn't like him," declared Freddie.

At this very moment Dinah, having finished hanging up the towels, stepped backward. She did not see Waggo. He saw her but was too close to avoid her. There was nothing for him to do but run between her feet!

Dinah lost her balance. She swayed a moment,

then *plunk,* she sat down hard upon the ground.

"Oh! Oh!" cried Flossie and Freddie, dashing up to her. "Are you hurt, Dinah?"

Dinah was not hurt by her fall but the breath had been knocked out of her.

"Waggo, you're a bad dog!" scolded Flossie. The little terrier paid no attention. He himself was having a hard time, for he had tripped on the clown suit and taken a somersault. By the time he got to the back fence, no one was there.

Waggo came back to the twins and whined. Flossie was sure he wanted the suit taken off, and she was right. The instant he was free, Waggo ran to the fence and tried to jump over.

"Somethin' out dere he don't like," said Dinah.

The small twins opened the gate and looked out, while Freddie held on to Waggo's collar. Far off they could see a gray cat streaking away at top speed.

"All that fuss over a little old cat!" exclaimed Freddie. But he laughed and patted Waggo. "You certainly scared him off, old fellow." Then he tied Waggo to the gate and told him to behave.

But Waggo was young and too full of fun to stay quiet long. After the twins had gone into the house he worked and worked to slip the collar over his head. Usually Waggo wore a leather harness. But he had ruined it while swimming, so Bert had put his old collar back on.

The collar was cracked in several places. In a few minutes it gave way to the dog's tugging. Waggo, unnoticed by any of the Bobbseys, went tearing down the street in search of more excitement.

A few minutes later Bert Bobbsey came along, carrying his new purchase. He was very proud to own the ship model of the schooner *Spray,* and was sure it was worth much more than the two dollars he had paid for it.

"Sure swell of Mr. Lenter to let me buy the model," the boy mused, turning into the Bobbsey driveway.

As he walked into the kitchen, Dinah looked at the ship with interest.

"Dat sho' is pretty, Bert," she said. "But my, my, what a lot o' dust! Yo' bettah take it outside till it gets cleaned off!"

Bert went out to the yard. "I'll put it in the garage," he decided.

As Bert walked into the garage, glancing out the window he saw a boy sneak through the gate in the back fence. It was Danny Rugg! Bert stepped outside, and Danny paused. Then he caught sight of the ship model and stared.

"Where'd you get that ship?" he demanded in surly tones.

"I bought it," Bert answered shortly.

"How much?"

"Why do you want to know?" Bert asked.

" 'Cause I'm going to buy it from you."

"This model isn't for sale!" Bert declared in a firm voice.

"Why not?" Danny Rugg demanded, walking toward Bert. "I told Mr. Lenter I wanted this model. He had no right to sell it to you!"

Bert became angry.

"Mr. Lenter said you never came back for it."

"I was going to this very day," Danny blustered. "You've got to give it to me!"

"You're too late. And I'll tell you something else, Danny Rugg! The sooner you get out of my yard, the better it will be for you!"

"Oh, is that so?" sneered the young bully. "Now I'll tell *you* something! If you don't sell that model to me, I'll—I'll—"

"You'll what?" interrupted Bert.

Danny did not answer but advanced toward Bert. The bully had a stick in his right hand!

CHAPTER III

GATHERING TOYS

"PUT that stick down!" demanded Bert. "If you want to fight, fight fair!"

Danny Rugg kept tight hold of the stick. Bert set down the ship model and stood still. Suddenly Danny raised his arm and leaped forward. Bert dodged, but grabbed the bully's legs, so that he went flat on the ground.

"Wowee!" shouted a voice from the house.

It was Freddie, who came running to help his brother in the fight. But Danny had had enough for the moment. He picked himself up and, muttering that he would get square, went off through the gate.

Bert went into the garage and hid the *Spray* on a shelf behind two large watering cans. He planned to get some clean rags from Dinah and dust it off. But before he had a chance to do this, Mr. and Mrs. Bobbsey came home. Bert as well as the other children rushed up to them to ask about the toy shop.

"I'm going to fix fire engines," declared Freddie.

"And I'll paste dolls—real good, too," said Flossie.

Their parents laughed. They could not make any sense out of what the twins were trying to tell them.

"Don't you think it would be all right for Nan and me to help Uncle Linn in his toy shop?" Bert asked.

"It's for children who have no toys of their own," Nan added.

"I know Mr. Smith is very good at mending toys," said Mr. Bobbsey. "I understand he's going to send some to children in other parts of the country."

"He won't be able to do that unless we help him," said Nan.

"Why not?" her mother asked.

Nan explained how the toy mender had broken his wrist.

"That's where we come in," said Bert, "if you'll let us, Dad and Mother. Uncle Linn wants us to do the work. He'll show us how."

Mr. and Mrs. Bobbsey looked at each other and then nodded.

"If Uncle Linn thinks you can do the job, I

guess it will be all right," said the twins' father. "Only," he added, looking at Flossie and Freddie, "I'm afraid my Fat Fairy and my Little Fireman had better not do much."

Mr. Bobbsey often called the small twins by these nicknames. Whenever he did, they knew he was not being especially stern about what he was saying. So now they knew he did not mean that they could not help at all in the toy shop. Rather, Flossie and Freddie understood they were not to get into mischief.

"I—I got muscles," said Freddie, flexing his arm and showing a bulging muscle the way he had seen one of the men at Mr. Bobbsey's lumber-yard do.

The rest of the family laughed, and Mr. Bobbsey said Freddie's muscles certainly would come in handy carrying the toys that needed mending.

"You and Flossie ought to be able to collect broken toys from your friends," suggested Mrs. Bobbsey.

"I know where there's a horse without a head," declared Flossie. "I mean his head's one place and the rest of him's in a box. Maybe Uncle Linn could show Bert how to put him together."

The children could hardly wait to tell Mr.

Smith the good news that they had received permission to go into the toy-mending business. But since Aunt Sallie had said to come back the next day, Mrs. Bobbsey insisted that they wait.

"But we can collect toys, and surprise Uncle Linn," said Nan.

"Bet I can get more'n anybody else," spoke up Freddie.

"Bet you can't," Flossie disagreed, and started off for the home of her friend Susie Larker to see what she could find.

"Don't be late to dinner," her mother called.

For the next two hours the twins kept busy. Bert and Nan, before starting out, discussed where they might locate some old toys no longer needed.

"We might try Mrs. Thorp and Mrs. Johnson," said Nan. "Their children are grown up now. Maybe some of their toys are still around."

"Good idea," Bert agreed. "You go around to Pine Street and call on Mrs. Thorp. I'll go through Elm and see Mrs. Johnson."

He left his twin sister at Pine Street, and kept on to the Johnson home. It was a large house with extensive grounds around it. The Johnson children used to play games on the lawn and swing on ropes tied to the tree branches. But now all the playthings were put away and everything was very quiet.

"Why, yes, Bert." Mrs. Johnson smiled, when the boy told her what he was after. "There are some toys in the attic you can have. Come with me."

Bert was delighted to find a good-looking Noah's Ark there. Although it was broken, as well as some of the animals that went in it, glue would make them almost as good as new. He also found roller skates which needed new wheels, a toy theater, and a miniature lighthouse.

"These will be fine after they're repaired," said Bert. "May I have them?"

"You surely may," Mrs. Johnson replied. "Put them in this basket and carry them downstairs. But be careful, the stairs are winding and steep."

"I sure will," Bert promised.

But he was not careful enough. Halfway down he slipped and the basket of toys flew from his hand.

"Oh, gosh!" Bert exclaimed.

"Are you hurt?" asked Mrs. Johnson anxiously.

"No. But I'm afraid the Noah's Ark animals are in pretty bad shape now," the boy answered.

Disgusted at his clumsiness, Bert picked them up one by one. Fortunately only two had been damaged. One he was sure could be mended, but a tiger was hopelessly smashed. Bert held onto the railing the rest of the way downstairs. He reached home without further mishap.

Nan, Flossie, and Freddie were already there. The younger twins were proudly showing off several broken toys their friends had given them for the toy shop. Flossie held up the headless horse.

"Bert, could you make a new head for him?" she asked. "Susie couldn't find his."

"Gee, I'm not that good." Bert laughed. "I'm only a toy mender, not a toy maker."

Flossie sighed. "Then Susie Larker will just *have* to find his head," she replied.

Freddie had brought an express wagon with all the sides and the handle missing.

"It doesn't 'express' any more," he explained. "It runs kind of slow. I'll oil her up."

"Don't oil it in the house," Bert said. "Wait till we get to Uncle Linn's."

Nan was mysterious about what she had brought from Mrs. Thorp's. Finally she pulled a whole set of miniature dancers from her pocket. Mrs. Bobbsey exclaimed in delight over them.

"These can hardly be called toys," she said. "They are precious! Look at that ballet dancer!"

"One leg's gone," said Flossie practically.

"And this Spanish dancer," Mrs. Bobbsey went on. "What a beautiful shawl! And she even has a high comb in her hair. Why, this is very old and valuable."

"Why is she valuable if she hasn't any arms?" Flossie wanted to know.

Her mother laughed. "Maybe you have a point there, my dear," she said. "Just the same, they're exquisite dolls."

"We should have 'squisite' things in our toy shop," Flossie persisted. "Please, Mother, let's put the dancers in!"

Dinah announced dinner and the family went into the dining room. During the meal, Bert told his parents about the model of the *Spray* he had bought.

"I'll show it to you when we finish," he said. "It's nifty, and I paid only two dollars for it."

Bert did not tell about Danny Rugg wanting it.

"I bet you could sell the ship for more'n two dollars," Freddie spoke up.

Bert said he wanted to keep it. Then he mentioned Mr. Lenter's hint that there was a mystery connected with the real ship *Spray*.

"Did you ever hear of the wreck of the *Spray,* Dad?" he asked.

"Oh, yes, I've heard about it."

"Was there a treasure on board?" Nan asked, her brown eyes eager.

"They never found out," her father answered. "Some people thought there must be, since the captain's fortune was never located after the *Spray* went down. But I don't think many people take much stock in that any more."

From where Bert sat at the table, he could look into the yard. It was growing dark, as if a storm were brewing. Suddenly something outside caught his eye.

"Excuse me, please," he said quickly, getting up from the table.

"What's the matter?" his mother asked.

But Bert was already in the kitchen. Stumbling past Dinah and Sam he dashed for the rear door. He had seen a bobbing flashlight near the garage. Someone was going in or coming out!

"Hi there!" the boy called. "Who are you?"

There was no answer, but someone started to run. Bert, fearful that his ship was being taken, raced after the prowler. But it was now too dark for him to make out the identity of the intruder.

"Stop!" Bert yelled, dashing out the back gate.

But the prowler had disappeared from view. Bert turned back and snapped on the garage light. He jumped up on a bench to look behind the watering cans, where he had hidden the ship. The model was not there!

"It's gone!" Bert cried aloud. "My ship model's gone!"

CHAPTER IV

THE OLD SAILOR

"WHAT'S goin' on heah? What's de trouble?" asked Sam, Dinah's husband, coming into the garage.

Bert was so angry and so shocked he could only stammer:

"The mean—I didn't think—he's the worst—"

"Bert, calm yo'self," said Sam. He was a mild-mannered, good-natured man. "Now tell me easy-like what's happened."

Bert explained how he had refused to sell the ship model to Danny Rugg, and now it was gone.

"But Danny can't get away with this!" Bert declared, jumping down from the bench. "I'll— Sam!" he cried suddenly. "Behind you!"

Sam turned around. On the floor in a front corner of the garage stood the *Spray!*

"Dat's just what I told you, Bert," said Sam. "Nuthin' to get so mad about."

"But who put the ship model down there?" Bert asked in amazement.

Sam could not answer this question, nor could anyone else in the Bobbsey household. But Bert was positive the figure he had seen sneaking around the garage was Danny Rugg. He concluded that Danny had got as far as the front of the garage when Bert had yelled at him. Then probably Danny, afraid he would be caught, had put down the *Spray* and raced off.

"Now, Bert," said Mr. Bobbsey, after he had heard why his son thought Danny was guilty, "you haven't the least proof that Danny was the person you saw. You must be very sure a person's guilty before—"

"But who else could it be?" Bert argued.

"I don't know," his father said, shrugging. "But since he didn't get the ship model, whoever he is, it's just possible he may be back. Tell you what you do," Mr. Bobbsey suggested. "Dust off the ship model right now, and take it up to your bedroom. It'll be safe there."

Bert grinned. "Sure thing, Dad."

Early the next morning, directly after breakfast, the Bobbsey twins set out for Uncle Linn's house. They found him eating pancakes, using his left hand. His right arm was in a cast. Aunt

Sallie Pry was fluttering around him like a hen mothering a chick.

"Good morning, good morning," the toy mender said cheerfully. Then he added with a wink toward his sister:

> *"My nurse makes me mind,*
> *But I'd rather play hooky*
> *With twins. We'd have fun,*
> *I'll bet a cookie!"*

The twins giggled. "We sure would," Bert declared.

"But Aunt Sallie's right making you take it easy," said Nan.

"Of course, I'm right baking cakes that aren't greasy," spoke up Aunt Sallie, who was not wearing her hearing aid.

As the children smiled at her mistake, Uncle Linn said, "Sallie, Sallie, such nonsense!"

His sister knew she had made some comical error, and asked Nan to go to the Pry house at once for the hearing device.

"We can help you in your toy shop, Uncle Linn," spoke up Freddie, who could not wait another minute to tell the news. "I want to start work."

"So your parents said it was all right, eh?" the toy mender beamed. "That's fine. But, Freddie, I'm afraid the jobs will be pretty hard for you and Flossie. Why don't you two just stick to collecting toys?"

The small twins were rather disappointed. But when Uncle Linn Smith told them what an important part of the work this was, they felt better.

"I haven't one-tenth enough toys to fill all my orders for the children around here and in other towns too," he said. "If you went out collecting every day for a month, it wouldn't be too much."

"Wowee!" said Freddie. "Come on, Floss. Let's get going."

Nan thought she had better accompany them, but the twins promised not to get into the busy section of Lakeport; just the neighborhood in which they lived. After they had left, Uncle Linn went to his toy shop with the older twins.

"We'll start on some simple things," he said. "How about this boat, Bert? It needs the masts glued on. I could do it in a minute, but it takes two hands. Hm," he went on, "those sails are pretty dirty. Nan, do you think you could put on clean ones?"

"Oh, yes," Nan assured him. "I'll get an old sheet from Aunt Sallie."

As Bert carefully set the masts in place and glued them, he told Uncle Linn about the ship model he had bought, and asked the old man if he had ever heard of the wreck of the *Spray*.

"My, yes," the toy mender answered. "It was in that same storm that my own little boat was wrecked. But that was a long time ago. Probably the *Spray* has broken up by this time. She was an old schooner, ridin' the river here even before I was born."

"You mean you don't think the *Spray* is still on the bottom where she went down?" Bert asked.

"Oh, maybe her hull's there," Uncle Linn replied. "Sunk deep in the mud, I venture. But the rest of her's probably rotted away. Remember, it happened a good many years ago. In fact, the captain's son was only seven or eight years old. He'd be about twenty-five now, I should think."

"What happened to the captain's son after the *Spray* went down?" Bert asked.

"Well, Bert," the old toy mender said slowly, "the boy's mother wasn't living, so he was sent away to some distant relatives out West. Too bad the money his father was supposed to have was never found."

Bert was thoughtful for a few minutes, as he carefully set the toy he had mended on a shelf. He had taken off the old sails so Nan could use them for a pattern. She had brought scissors, thread, and needles from the house; also a piece of canvas that Aunt Sallie had given her.

"Did you ever hear of a mystery about the *Spray?*" Bert asked the toy mender.

"Seems to me I did," Uncle Linn answered. "I don't just recall what it was."

"Wasn't there a treasure on board?" the boy said eagerly.

"There was some talk at the time that the captain may have had all his money with him, and it went down on the ship. But there was no proof, and you know, Bert, it costs money to send divers down. The captain's relatives had no money.

"The captain had some strange ideas," Uncle Linn went on. "For one thing, he didn't believe in putting his money in banks. That's why folks thought he must have kept it on the *Spray.*"

"Not everybody went down with the ship," said Bert. "Mr. Lenter told us the man who sold him the ship model was saved."

"Oh, you mean the fellow who calls himself Matey Foster? Some people say he didn't go on that ill-fated voyage at all. Captain fired him just before they started out. Well, there's no one alive to argue the matter."

Bert was puzzled. If the captain had not liked Matey Foster, how did it happen that the sailor had the model of the *Spray?*

"That was kind of queer," Uncle Linn admitted, when Bert asked him.

When Uncle Linn said the captain, being an excellent wood carver, probably had made the model himself, Bert was more pleased than ever to own it. After telling the toy mender how someone had moved the toy *Spray* in the garage, probably trying to steal it, Bert said:

"I thought it was Danny Rugg. Do you know anybody else who might want it?"

Uncle Linn shook his head. Suddenly Bert thought of something. He would ask Mr. Lenter if anyone had inquired about the model of the *Spray!*

Two hours later Aunt Sallie came out to say she thought her brother and the twins should stop work. Uncle Linn ought to rest, and the children should play in the sunshine.

"I guess you're right," the toy mender said.

He had been doing what he could with one hand and was tired. He praised Bert and Nan highly for their work.

"Look at that toy ship up there, Sallie," he pointed. "Good as new now. And that doll house. All ready for shipping. Bert nailed it together and fixed the broken chairs for it. Nan made some new curtains and rugs."

"Why, that's wonderful." Aunt Sallie praised the twins. "You'd better watch your step, Linn. They'll be putting you out of business!"

As there was still an hour left before lunch would be ready at the Bobbsey home, Bert decided to stop at Mr. Lenter's shop and see what he could find out. Nan said she would go on to Mrs. White's house to see if she had any toys. Mrs. White was a close friend of Mrs. Bobbsey.

Mrs. White opened the door herself and invited Nan inside. Nan told her of the need for more toys which could be fixed up and given to children who could not get them any other way.

"My second attic is full of them," Mrs. White said, smiling. "You may take all you want, Nan."

"Thank you very much," the girl replied. "Mrs. White, what do you mean by your *second* attic?"

"It's an attic within an attic," the gray-haired

woman laughed. "Perhaps you'd call it a big closet."

She took Nan to the third floor, and snapped on the light. In the outer attic were pieces of furniture, several boxes, suitcases, and a spinning wheel. Mrs. White wound her way among these until she came to a door. Nan followed. When Mrs. White opened the door, Nan could see all sorts of toys piled up beyond.

"Oh, this is wonderful!" she cried. "It's like finding a treasure."

"Nan, stay as long as you like and look the things over," Mrs. White told her. "Don't hurry. I was just going out. You don't mind being here alone, do you?"

"Oh, no."

"My sister's ill, so I'm going to her house for a few days," Mrs. White explained. "Mr. White's out of town, so it's a good time for me to go. Just let yourself out the front door, Nan. Good-bye. I'll have to hurry now to catch my train."

Nan had a lot of fun pulling the toys from the closet. Mrs. White had several children, now grown up, and there were toys for both boys and girls. Nan separated the perfect ones from those that needed mending. There were a fine drum and sticks. She almost wished they were broken!

"Whew! It's hot in here!" Nan told herself presently. "Guess I'll open that window."

There was just one small window in the room. It looked out on vacant property back of the White home. Nan had to tug hard at the catch before she could unfasten it.

"What a sweet doll's bed this is!" she thought, getting back to work. "And it needs mending, too. I'll take this."

Nan kept busy for half an hour. She did not notice that a stiff breeze had sprung up outside. Suddenly a strong gust blew the door shut with a loud bang.

"Oh!" said Nan. Then, looking out the window, she could see dark clouds in the sky. "It's going to rain. I'd better go home," she told herself.

Nan picked up the toys she had decided to take and went to the door. The handle turned easily, but the door would not budge.

At first Nan thought it was stuck. But though she pushed against it with all her might, she could not budge the door. Then the awful truth dawned on her. She tried not to cry.

"I'm—a prisoner—in this house!" she said, frightened.

CHAPTER V

BERT TO THE RESCUE

NAN pushed and pushed at the attic door. It would not budge. She tried the knob again. It spun round and round in her hand.

"Oh, dear, what am I going to do?" she asked herself.

Nan tried to be brave and sensible. Every door could be opened from the *inside,* she told herself. But this one just wouldn't open.

She did not know it, but the house was old, and when the attic door would not stay closed, Mr. White had put a latch on the outside of it. The hard bang of the door, when the wind shut it, had made the latch settle into place. Someone would have to lift the latch to let Nan Bobbsey out.

The girl ran to the window and shouted, "Let me out! Let me out! I'm locked in Mrs. White's attic!"

She looked down and waited. No one came

in sight. Again she cried out as loudly as she could.

"Help! Help! Please come and let me out! I'm in Mrs. White's attic!"

Still there was no answer. No sound of approaching footsteps.

Nan called again. Finally she realized that she was not being heard. The window opened on the rear of the property, which was deserted.

"But someone will surely come soon," she told herself, shouting until she was hoarse.

Finally Nan gave up. Tears rolled down her cheeks as she realized that even if someone heard her, he could not get into the house to let her out of her prison.

Mr. and Mrs. White, who had the keys, would be out of town for several days!

Nan had a wild idea that she might make a rope from some of the old clothes in the attic and climb down that way from the window. But when she saw how far it was to the ground, she gave up such a dangerous plan.

"What'll I do? What'll I do?" she thought helplessly.

As Nan sat down on a suitcase to think things out, her eye lighted on the drum and sticks.

"I'll drum a call for help!" she said excitedly. Nan had beat on Bert's and Freddie's drums many times.

Nan grabbed up the drum and sticks and ran to the window. She hung the drum around her neck by the cord and, holding it out of the window, began to beat on it as loudly as she could.

Dr—ub! Dr—ub! Dr-r-r-r-ub!

The throbbing sound echoed loudly. Resting a moment, Nan looked down into the yard. No one was in sight.

Again she plied the sticks with all her might. The drum was really rattling now!

Not many people were around, but coming along the back street was the very person to help Nan Bobbsey. Her twin!

Bert was on his way to see Danny Rugg. Hearing the drum, he stopped and listened. The boy smiled to himself. The drummer was not very good; just about as good as his sister Nan.

"Nan!" Bert said, half aloud. Realizing he was near Mrs. White's house, he laughed. "I'll bet it *is* Nan. She's found a drum for our toy shop!"

Bert scooted across the open property back of Mrs. White's house. He was surprised to see the drum hanging out the window, and stood still. Nan stopped beating it and looked out again.

"Bert!" she cried. "Oh, Bert, I'm locked in! Get me out!"

Quickly Nan told her brother what had happened. He dashed to several houses in the neighborhood to see if anyone had a key to the Whites' house. No one did.

"I know what!" Bert thought suddenly. "Those painters I saw!"

On the next block two men were painting a house. When Bert told them his story, they put a long ladder on their truck and drove to where Nan was a prisoner. Then they set the ladder against the house up to the attic window.

"Do you think you can make it, little girl?" one of the painters called up.

"Oh, yes," Nan cried in relief. "But first I'd like to have these toys taken down. Bert, can you come up?"

"Sure."

Bert climbed the long ladder, and Nan handed him the doll's bed. On the way down, he dropped the covers and mattress out, but this did not matter.

Nan tossed a rag doll, a football, and a clown

suit to the painters, who caught them expertly. Then she let herself out of the window, closed it, and went down the ladder. As she reached the ground, the rain suddenly started to come down hard.

"Jump in the truck, children," one of the painters ordered. "I'll run you home."

Nan, Bert, and the toys were soon at the Bobbsey house. When Flossie heard how her sister had been locked in, she shivered a little and said:

"Oh, I'd have been awful scared!"

"I was kind of scared myself until Bert came," Nan confessed.

Freddie felt bad that he had not been the one to have the adventure. Next to being rescued from a burning building on a fireman's ladder, climbing down from an attic on a painter's ladder would have been most exciting.

"Well, I'm certainly glad you're safe, Nan," said Mrs. Bobbsey with a sigh. "We might not have found you for days. And now, let's have lunch. Dinah's had it ready for an hour."

By the time the Bobbseys had eaten, the rain had stopped. Bert decided to go find Danny Rugg. Mr. Lenter had said no one had asked about the ship model of the *Spray* after Bert bought it.

"So the person who tried to take my ship model must be Danny," Bert argued with himself.

He strode off to where the Ruggs lived. He found Danny teasing a gray cat that was meowing angrily. As Bert approached, he saw that Danny had the cat by its tail. The cat spit and yowled but could not get free.

"Hey, what's the idea?" called Bert.

Danny turned around, but he did not let go of the cat.

"None of your business," the mean boy answered.

"You have no right to hurt animals!" Bert declared hotly.

"Aw, I'm not hurting her," Danny said. "She's not a sissy like you!"

But he let the cat go and ran up on the porch, as Bert started for him.

"Take that back!" Bert cried out.

"What?" asked Danny, as if he did not know that calling Bert a sissy would make him furious.

"You know what I mean!"

Danny probably would not have taken back what he had said, if he could have run into the house. But the door was locked.

"Oh, all right," he said grudgingly. "Now go on home!"

Bert thought Danny had a frightened look on his face, and he had never known him to give up so easily.

"Not before we settle something," said Bert. "You came sneaking around our garage last night, didn't you?"

Danny did not answer.

"Listen here," said Bert. "You can't have that ship model!"

"Who said I took your old ship?" Danny asked angrily. *"I did not!"*

"I didn't say you did," Bert replied quickly, "but you were sneaking around where it was. Well, I'm just warning you not to try taking it!"

As Bert walked off, Danny looked after him angrily.

"I couldn't even find it when I was there," he thought. "I'll fix Bert Bobbsey for this!"

Bert went directly to Uncle Linn's toy shop. The other twins were there, busy at work. The old toy mender was trying with one hand to help Freddie mend the hose in his broken fire engine.

"If we can fix this engine so it squirts," said Freddie, "I can send it anywhere to put out fires."

"Good for you!" exclaimed Uncle Linn. Then with a smile he added:

"When the fire begins to burn,
Then it is the engine's turn.
It squirts the water up so high,
It seems to reach right to the sky."

"I wish my fire engine could squirt to the sky," Freddie laughed. "Only then I'd never give it away."

Freddie soon grew tired of his job and turned it over to Bert. The small twin wandered to a corner to see what Flossie was doing.

"I'm gluing heads and arms and legs on some wooden soldiers," said Flossie. "They're broken off. They must have been in a big fight."

"That's man's work," declared Freddie, starting to take one of the soldiers away from her.

"Stop!" said his twin. "I guess soldiers are 'portant to me, too. Why don't you paint that wagon over there?"

Freddie thought this was a grand idea. He found some bright-red paint and started work. Unfortunately, Uncle Linn, Bert, and Nan were too busy to notice that he set the open can of paint on the edge of a bench alongside Flossie.

Just as he started to work, Flossie's right hand became stuck to a piece of wood. As she pulled it loose, her hand flew up and struck Freddie's arm.

Freddie was just dipping his brush into the can of paint. Instantly it went over.

The little boy tried to jump away. But his foot slipped and he fell to the floor. The can of red paint fell on top of him!

CHAPTER VI

FIRE ALARM

WHAT a sight Freddie Bobbsey was! Red paint from head to toe!

"Golly!" exclaimed Bert, rushing over to him.

"Don't touch your face, Freddie!" cried Nan. "You'll get paint in your eyes!"

"Oh, Freddie!" wailed Flossie. "It was all my fault!"

Red paint was running all over the floor! The others tried not to step in it, as they went to the little boy's aid.

"It was just an accident," said Nan kindly. "But you are a mess, Freddie. We'd better go home."

"Let me take care of him," said Uncle Linn. "I'll clean his clothes with turpentine. When I get paint on myself, that's what I use."

"I'll go home and get him some clean things," Nan offered. "Can you get the paint off his face and hands, Uncle Linn?"

"Oh, yes, I can clean them with turpentine, too."

"You'll do nothing of the sort," said a voice from the doorway.

The speaker was Aunt Sallie, who immediately took charge of Freddie Bobbsey. She had often taken care of the twins, and the little boy did not object. In fact, he would be very glad to get the paint off as soon as possible!

Aunt Sallie told the little boy to leave his pants, socks, shirt, and shoes with Uncle Linn, who was sprinkling sawdust over the paint on the floor. Then she hustled him into the house, shampooed his hair, and got all the paint from his face and hands. Nan brought a fresh supply of clothes for him.

"Such a time!" sighed Aunt Sallie. "You made me forget why I went out to the toy shop. I brought a jigsaw puzzle. A woman left it here. She said a few of the pieces are missing, but new ones could be made. Then it'll be perfect."

Mrs. Pry had set the box containing the puzzle on a shelf in the toy shop. Nan hurried out to find it. When the girl read "Four hundred pieces" on the box, she said, "Oh, dear!"

"What's the matter?" Bert called.

Nan explained that it would be necessary to

put the puzzle together in order to find out what pieces were missing. And there were four hundred of them!

"It'll take a long time to do that," she said.

"We'll all work on it," spoke up Uncle Linn. Then he chuckled. "Only I find working on a jigsaw puzzle is like eating peanuts. You can't stop!"

The toy mender set up a table, and dumped the pieces of the puzzle onto it. The four twins crowded around, and the work started. Nan found the first two pieces that fit. By the end of an hour most of the pieces were in place. Only part of the center was not finished.

"I guess we'll call it a day," said the toy mender, who was very tired. "We've all done a lot of work. I'm proud of my helpers." He smiled. "I'm sure the Bobbsey twins' toy shop will be a big success."

"I declare," he went on as he looked at the mended toys, and those still in need of repair which he and the twins had collected, "this toy shop is almost as good as the one Mr. Hewson runs on Main Street."

Hewson's was the biggest store in Lakeport, and turned over its broken toys to Uncle Linn to fix and give away.

"By the way, Mr. Hewson has a load for us right now," Uncle Linn said.

"I'll go get them in a couple of days," Bert offered.

The children felt very proud and happy as they went home. Their parents asked how things were going.

"We had one accident today," Flossie reported. "But maybe that was good. It got Freddie a shampoo."

Mr. and Mrs. Bobbsey laughed. It was a family joke that Freddie hated to have his hair washed by any method except a swim.

Bert was up early the next morning. He decided to go to the toy shop ahead of the others and finish the puzzle, so he could make the new pieces. While Dinah cooked his breakfast, he talked to her about Danny, and said the boy denied having been the one who tried to take the ship model from the garage.

"You don't suppose it could have been dat sailorman?" Dinah asked.

"What! A sailor!" cried Bert, remembering Matey Foster, who had sold the ship model to Mr. Lenter.

"He looked lak one," said Dinah. "Tight pants, middy blouse—"

"Where was he?" asked Bert quickly.

"Lookin' in our garage," the cook replied. "Sam asked him what he wanted. He said he didn't want nuthin', and went off."

Bert was so excited that Dinah had to remind him not to eat so fast.

"Yo'll go get yo'self a stomach-ache, and no boat nor no sailor's worth dat."

"What'd he look like?" Bert asked eagerly.

"Goodness, chile, I don't know. They all look alike to me in those sailor suits."

"What ship is he on?"

"Chile, how would I know dat? And Sam don't neither, I guess."

"Well, anyway, the ship model's safe in my room, so nobody can steal it now," said Bert. But he still did not like the idea of strangers sneaking around their house.

As soon as he had eaten, the boy hurried off to Uncle Linn's toy shop. Thinking about it made him grin. Uncle Linn had called it the Bobbsey twins' toy shop!

"I wonder how many pieces of that puzzle are missing," he asked himself, swinging open the door of the old barn. "If there are a lot—"

Bert stood still and gaped. The puzzle was no longer on the table! The table had been tipped over. A few pieces of the puzzle lay scattered on the floor, but the rest of them were gone.

As the boy looked around, he saw other pieces lying here and there in the barn. Someone had deliberately thrown them about, one by one.

Bert gathered up all he could find, getting madder all the time. What mean person had done this? His first thought was, of course, Danny Rugg, but there was no way to prove this.

"Meow! Meow!" wailed a cat suddenly.

Bert gazed around. He could not see it.

"Meow!" cried the cat louder.

The boy was puzzled. Was Uncle Linn hiding and playing a joke on him? Just then the toy mender appeared and said he had not been imitating a cat. He helped Bert search for it. Finally they found the animal in a carton under one of the benches.

"Looks like Danny Rugg's kind of joke," said Bert. "He enjoys hurting cats."

He told about Danny tormenting the cat the day before, then about the puzzle having been thrown around. Uncle Linn agreed it did seem likely that Danny was guilty of both tricks. But the toy mender advised Bert not to let the bully know he had been upset.

"If you pretend you don't suspect him, maybe he'll give himself away," said Uncle Linn.

"I'll try," Bert agreed, "but it's going to be hard."

He put Danny out of his mind, set the cat free, and started all over again to fix the jigsaw puzzle. It was easier this time, because he remembered parts of the picture. Nan came in a little later and helped him. Finally, with Uncle Linn working too, they got all the pieces in place.

"It's Santa Claus and his reindeer!" Nan exclaimed. "Only Donner's head's gone."

"And one of Blitzen's legs," laughed Bert.

Altogether, ten of the four hundred wooden pieces were missing. Bert said he could cut new ones on the jigsaw, but he never could make the picture to be pasted on them. Nan, and even Uncle Linn, felt unequal to the task.

"I know who could." The toy maker smiled. "My sister Sallie."

Nan ran off to tell Aunt Sallie. "Why, I haven't painted in years," she protested. But she agreed to try fixing up the missing pieces.

While the work was going on, Flossie came racing into the shop. She was very much excited.

"Look what I brought!" she cried. "Isn't she be-yootiful, even if her hair's gone?"

Flossie proudly showed a doll about a foot high. It had a beautiful face but looked strange without a wig.

"Her eyes," exclaimed Nan. "They're just like—like beautiful jewels."

Uncle Linn was very much interested. He had never seen a doll like this one. It was exquisitely made, and though its clothes were torn, they were of very fine material. Aunt Sallie declared the lace trimming was handmade.

"And those eyes! Their centers look like real sapphires," she said. "But, of course, they must be just glass."

Flossie insisted that Uncle Linn give her new doll his special attention. So the kindly toy mender got out a box of doll wigs. The little girl tried them on the doll one at a time. Most of them looked very strange, but at last Flossie found one that was meant for a lady doll, and this one looked very well on her.

"She's a queen," said Aunt Sallie in admiration. "That's why her clothes are so beautiful. Where did you get her?"

"From Mrs. Randall's little girl. She found

it in some trash outside a house," Flossie answered.

"I think," said Aunt Sallie, "that this was once a valuable doll."

"Then we ought to fix her up for some very special girl," Flossie announced.

"That's a good idea," called Uncle Linn, pleased. "Sallie, how about helping me fix her now?"

"Well, all right, but I was going to bake some cookies for the Bobbsey twins, and make an apple pie for you, and—" His sister paused, her eyes twinkling merrily.

Uncle Linn laughed and said, "Then the doll can wait."

"Sure," said Bert. "Please make the cookies, Aunt Sallie. That chocolate kind with the nuts on top."

"Oh, you mean the Aunt Sallie Special," said Mrs. Pry.

She went off to do the baking. A few minutes later Freddie arrived with an armful of toy animals to be repaired. As he laid them on a bench, the town's fire whistle began to blow. The children counted the number of blasts. One, two, three, four! One, two, three!

"Forty-three!" shouted Freddie excitedly.

The little fireman felt in his pants pocket for a certain card. He found it—a card telling where the locations of the fire numbers were. Long ago a fireman had given it to Freddie, and he always carried it with him.

"Main and River!" he announced.

"Main and River?" Bert repeated. "That's where Hewson's Toy Shop is. Do you suppose—"

The Bobbsey twins ran from Uncle Linn's barn. He went after the children as fast as he could but was unable to catch up to them.

As they neared the scene of the fire, Bert kept tight hold of Freddie, who was apt to lose his head. Nan held Flossie's hand.

"It *is* Hewson's!" cried Bert, as he saw smoke coming from the doorway.

"Oh, dear," said Flossie, "all the broken toys he was going to give us will be burned up!"

CHAPTER VII

RUTHIE WATSON

"I'M GOING to get my toy engine!" exclaimed Freddie as he saw the smoke rolling from Mr. Hewson's toy store.

"They wouldn't let you near enough to use it," said Bert. "Here, keep hold of my hand."

"Aw, I'm big enough—" began the small twin, pulling away. But Bert grasped his brother's hand tightly.

Flames suddenly burst from a basement window. Billows of smoke followed.

"The fire must have got a good start," Bert called to Nan. "I guess they can't save much."

Many pieces of fire apparatus had now reached the toy shop. A big crowd was gathering.

"Hey you, get back!" boomed a voice.

It was Policeman Kelly. He ordered everyone back, but the twins managed to stay in the front row of onlookers, where they could see the firemen, the lines of hose, and the streams of water.

"Golly! This is a swell place!" said Bert. "You ought to be satisfied, Freddie."

"I am." The little fellow was watching the throbbing pump of the engine. "I wish I had one like that," he said.

"It looks as if the whole store would burn up," remarked a man next to the twins. "Those painted toys and light playthings burn like tinder."

"It's too bad," Nan sighed. "Lots of children in Lakeport will have to go without toys, I guess."

With the calls of the firemen, the shouts of the crowd, the crackle of the fire, and the noise of the motors, the scene was now one of great excitement.

"Oh, look!" said Flossie. "They're bringing toys out!"

From an alleyway alongside the shop, firemen and several other men were carrying out rocking horses, doll carriages, little wagons, play pens, and garden swings.

"Maybe they'll save a lot," Nan said hopefully.

"Not much, I'm afraid," replied the man next to her. "It's a sad sight to see so many good toys go up in smoke."

At this moment Uncle Linn found the twins. He shook his head sadly.

"This is a great loss for Mr. Hewson," he said. "I wish I could do something for him."

Presently Mr. Hewson himself walked from the alley. Seeing Uncle Linn, he came over. The toy mender told him how sorry he was about the fire.

"Yes, it's awful," the owner replied. "But I'm not going to let it put me out of business. I understand you have a big barn, Mr. Smith."

"Yes, I have."

"Could you spare me room in it to store some new toys that are coming by express tomorrow?"

"Surely. Glad to."

"Then I'll have them taken to your barn. Thanks."

"What are you going to do with the things the firemen are bringing out now?" Nan asked Mr. Hewson.

"Give them to Mr. Smith, I guess. I never could sell them; they're blackened from smoke, and the paint on them's blistered."

"You're very kind," said Uncle Linn. "You can have the whole second floor of my barn. Why don't you open a store there?"

"Maybe I will. Thank you very much."

Mr. Hewson went off to tell the expressman, who had stopped to watch the fire, to deliver all the toys to Uncle Linn's place.

Although the blaze in the toy store was finally brought under control, much damage had been done. It was an excited pair of twins who arrived at the Bobbsey home a little later and told about the fire. Bert spoke of the extra toys coming to Uncle Linn's barn.

"We're going to have a very 'stensive business," Flossie said, when she could get a word in. "Upstairs and downstairs."

"Sounds like a very busy place," said Mr. Bobbsey.

Indeed, there was hustle and bustle at Uncle Linn's toy shop the next day. Aunt Sallie and the twins cleared out the second floor, carrying tools, peach baskets, and old harness to the cellar of Uncle Linn's house.

"I don't see," the toy mender grumbled, as he looked on, "why I had to go and break my wrist at this time." But he did what he could with one hand.

By noon the place was in order. The expressman brought the first load, and also a pile of lumber. Two of Mr. Hewson's clerks came and built some tables and shelves. Then they unpacked the toys. By six o'clock the second-floor toy store was ready for business!

"My, my, such a time!" said Aunt Sallie, as she wearily shooed the Bobbsey twins home.

They, too, were weary and slept soundly that night. But the next morning they arrived at Uncle Linn's barn early to begin work.

"I'm going upstairs and see the firsthand toy shop," said Flossie. "Then I'll come down and work on secondhand dolls." Flossie was specializing in dolls.

All the children climbed the stairs and were amazed to find two customers already there. One of them was Danny Rugg. He was riding a bicycle around.

"Well, son, do you want it?" the clerk was saying to him.

"I don't know yet," Danny answered. "I have to ride it a little longer."

"You've been riding it for fifteen minutes now," the man told him. "Make up your mind!"

The Bobbseys were sure that Danny did not intend to buy the bicycle. He had a good one of his own. But they said nothing and soon went downstairs.

Freddie and Flossie decided to go out and

collect more toys. Flossie had been promised a set of Eskimo dolls.

Bert and Nan got to work putting their toy shop in order. The things from the burned store were cluttering up the place.

"Let's put all the toys of one kind together," Nan suggested. "I'll collect all the dolls and doll houses and doll clothes," she said.

"Okay," Bert agreed. "I'll put the wagons and tricycles and everything else you can ride on in one place."

While they were busy, a little girl came hobbling into the toy shop on crutches. Nan immediately stopped working and spoke to her.

"I'm Ruthie Watson," the little girl said, smiling. "May I see Mr. Smith?"

"He's not here," Nan answered. "I think he went to the doctor's. Can I give him a message?"

Ruthie looked around the shop. "Oh, there are lots and lots more toys than when I was here before."

Nan explained how the extra toys happened to be there, and why the Bobbsey twins were helping Uncle Linn.

"I'm sorry to hear about his broken wrist," said Ruthie, "but it's going to be all right again." She looked down at her own crippled legs. "Not like me," she added sadly. "I'm never going to walk again without crutches."

Tears came to Nan Bobbsey's eyes. She said that maybe someday a fine doctor could help Ruthie.

"Maybe," said the crippled child, "if my daddy had a lot of money, he could find a doctor." Then suddenly she smiled. "But my mother says I mustn't think about it. Tomorrow's my birthday and I must be happy. Uncle Linn said he would give me a toy for my birthday."

Nan decided right then and there that she would give Ruthie something too. Maybe a sewing kit she had, with tricky little gadgets to help people who did not sew well.

"Why don't you look around and decide what toy you'd like?" Nan suggested kindly. "I'm sure Uncle Linn will be here soon."

"All right," said Ruthie.

Nan introduced her to Bert, then the crippled girl started a tour of the toy shop, while the twins went on with their work. None of them noticed a figure sneaking down the stairway.

It was Danny Rugg, who had not bought the bicycle or anything else on the second floor. He was smiling, a mean sort of smile.

"Now's my chance to get square with Bert Bobbsey!" he told himself.

Tiptoeing the rest of the way, he went to a corner of the twins' toy shop and helped himself to a velocipede. Though it was a large one, still it was too small for him. Nevertheless, he got on, and started at a fast clip down the aisle toward the door.

Bert spied him. Just as he yelled at Danny to get off, there came a crash and a scream.

Little Ruthie Watson had come around the corner. Danny hit her hard. The crutches flew from under the girl's arms, and she crumpled up on the floor.

CHAPTER VIII

THE GOOD-LUCK COIN

"RUTHIE!" exclaimed Nan Bobbsey. She ran over to the crippled girl, who lay groaning on the floor. "You're hurt!"

Meanwhile, Danny Rugg had jumped from the velocipede and was leaping toward the door. Bert stopped the bully and held fast to him.

"You're not going to run away!" cried Bert sternly.

"Let go of me!" Danny demanded, shoving the other boy off.

But Bert said Danny would have to do something about the accident he had caused, and do it fast. Danny was frightened.

"I didn't mean to do it," he whined. "I couldn't help it."

Again he tried to get away. At this moment Uncle Linn and Aunt Sallie came into the toy shop. How glad Bert and Nan were to see them!

Aunt Sallie at once took charge of Ruthie,

and with Nan's help carried her to the house. Aunt Sallie asked Nan to telephone Dr. Benson and then go for Mrs. Watson, who had no telephone.

Uncle Linn told Danny his parents would have to pay for any treatments needed to make Ruthie well again. The boy turned very pale, and Bert was afraid Danny might be too scared to go home. Uncle Linn must have had the same thought, because he made Danny wait there until he had telephoned Mr. Rugg to come over.

Mr. Rugg and Dr. Benson arrived at the same time. Danny was told to go home and stay there. Then his father and the doctor went into the house. They were inside a long while. Nan came back with Ruthie's mother, who also went inside.

"What do you suppose is happening?" Nan asked Bert, after twenty minutes had gone by. "It looks as if poor Ruthie's badly hurt."

"I'd like to punch Danny!" Bert said.

Finally Aunt Sallie came out and told them the story. One of Ruthie's legs had had to be treated and bandaged by the doctor. But what he had said afterward was very exciting. There was a chance that the little girl might someday walk again without crutches! There was a fine surgeon in New York who had done wonderful things for other children who were lame. Dr. Benson would try to make arrangements to have Ruthie go and see the surgeon.

When Nan and Bert were allowed to see Ruthie, she was lying on Aunt Sallie's bed. Uncle Linn asked her what toy she wanted from the shop.

"Oh, may I have the doll with the sparkling blue eyes and the beautiful clothes?" Ruthie asked.

"You certainly may."

Nan went out to get the doll, and Ruthie hugged it tightly.

"I'll keep her with me every minute," she said, smiling.

As the twins went back to the toy shop, Nan asked Uncle Linn what had happened to Danny.

"Mr. Rugg said Danny's punishment would be that he must sell his bicycle, and the money would be used to pay the doctor," Uncle Linn answered. "If Danny wants another bicycle, he'll have to earn the money for it. That ought to keep the lad out of mischief for a while!"

Bert grinned. "That's a swell idea!"

A moment later the younger Bobbsey twins hurried into the barn. Both were excited about their morning's collection of toys. Freddie was carrying a toy fire engine in one arm, and dragging another with his free hand.

"Aren't they swell!" he exclaimed. "But one of 'em has a busted hose. I'm going to fix it."

"I brought the Eskimo dolls," said Flossie, who was carrying them in a big paper bag. "Mrs. Frawley gave them to me. Her father was a sailor. He went to Eskimo Land, where we went once, and brought back these dolls."

"Oh, how cute!" cried Nan, as her sister took the dolls from the bag and stood them in a row on one of the benches.

"It's a whole family," Flossie explained. "That's the father, and the mother, and their boy Chan."

The others thought Flossie very smart to remember the boy doll's name. She surprised them still further by saying the daughter's name was Chi Chi, and the dog's Chingook.

"All the family's dressed in fur," said Nan. "Real sealskin."

"They must be terrible hot," said Flossie. "I think I'll take off their fur dresses, so they'll cool off. Sealskin's too warm."

Uncle Linn laughed. Then he said:

"What does a lady seal
Do when it's warm?
Store her fur coat,
Till the next snowstorm?"

The Bobbsey twins giggled, then settled down to work. There was silence for several minutes. Then Flossie exclaimed:

"Oh, look at this! I found a penny in Chi Chi's pocket!"

She held up a coin.

"That isn't a penny," remarked Uncle Linn, when he looked at it. "It's some foreign coin."

As the other children crowded around, Flossie said, "It's mine. Finder's keeper!"

"We'd better ask Mrs. Frawley about this," Nan remarked. "It may be a valuable coin."

She went to the telephone in Uncle Linn's house and called Mrs. Frawley. After Nan had described the coin, Mrs. Frawley said:

"Oh, yes, I remember. My father said the doll is called a good-luck doll. The coin is part of her costume, and brings good luck, too. I suppose some Eskimo father got the coin from a whaler, and gave it to his child to bring her extra luck."

"Don't you want it back?" Nan asked.

"No, you may keep it," Mrs. Frawley said.

"Maybe it will bring your toy shop good luck. You children and Uncle Linn are doing a fine piece of work."

"Thank you very much," said Nan.

When Flossie heard the story, she agreed to give up the coin and leave it in the pocket of the doll's dress.

"But the doll has to go to somebody that needs luck," she insisted.

"Well, I know someone who does," spoke up Nan quickly, and told the small twins about Ruthie Watson, and what had happened at the toy shop.

Flossie wanted to see the lame girl at once and give her the Eskimo dolls. Ruthie was just about to be taken from Aunt Sallie's house in a taxi. When the dolls were handed to her, she thought a moment, then said:

"I've just had a lot of good luck. See, I have the lovely queen doll. Thank you, Flossie, but I'd rather you'd give the Eskimo dolls to someone else who needs luck."

The twins could not think of another child at the moment, so after Ruthie had gone, they went back to the toy shop, and put Chi Chi, Chan, and their parents, together with Chingook the dog, on a shelf.

Flossie started work mending some paper dolls. There was a whole box of fancy clothes for them, which she sorted out. Half an hour later, as she was gluing some of them, Freddie shouted:

"It'll work now!"

The others, busy with their own jobs, did not pay any attention to the little boy. He went to the sink, got a pail of water, and filled the tank of the toy fire engine he had been working on. Then, holding the hose, he aimed it toward the sink.

Next, he started the pump going. There was a whirr from the spring, the grinding of wheels, and a moment later, a loud scream from Flossie.

"Oh, oh!" she cried. "Stop!"

"What happened?" shouted Nan, who was on the other side of the old barn.

"I'm all wet!" cried poor Flossie. "Freddie squirted water on me!"

A stream continued to pour from the hose of the toy fire engine. The force of the water had knocked the hose from Freddie's hands. All sorts of paper toys were getting soaked.

"Turn it off!" shouted Bert, running forward.

"I—I can't—the pump won't stop!" cried

Freddie, who was trying hard to turn a little handle.

Bert jumped to the toy engine, and aimed the little hose out an open window.

"Look what you did to me, Freddie Bobbsey!" said Flossie, who had caught the full force of the water. "I'm sopping wet!"

"I'm sorry!" said Freddie. "But—"

"And look at these paper dolls. They're all dripping!"

"I'm afraid they're ruined," said Nan. "And these paper trains, too."

The whole section of the shop where the paper toys were was indeed a sorry mess!

CHAPTER IX

THE TALL SHADOW

THE paper toys did seem to be in bad shape, but Uncle Linn was certain some of them could be dried out and used. He picked up the ones made of cardboard and shook the water from them.

"But these dolly dresses," wailed Flossie. "We can't fix them."

The toy mender, laughing, said the paper dresses could be a crinkled variety.

"A new style for dolls," he told Flossie.

After the wet mess had been cleaned up, it was found that very few toys were ruined after all. Freddie felt better, and promised to be more careful in the future.

After dinner that evening, Mr. Bobbsey told the twins he had a surprise. He showed Bert and Nan a small shadow theater a man had given him for the twins' toy shop. Its two sides would have to be repaired before it could be used for shows.

"This shadow theater," Mr. Bobbsey told the children, "is a copy of a very old one invented by the Chinese."

"The Chinese?" said Bert in amazement.

"Yes. The Chinese shadow theater was in use before regular theaters. And even before the use of puppets."

The shadow theater had a canvas screen in it. The person who put on the show crouched below this. He held up little cutout cardboard figures and bits of scenery attached to sticks. A light behind them caused their shadows to be shown on the screen.

"Let's mend this right away and try it out!" cried Nan enthusiastically.

Bert took the wooden framework to his workbench in the cellar and nailed it together. Then he put on a show with a policeman and a tramp. Next Nan made one up, using a farmer and a horse.

"It's pretty good," said Bert, "but I think we ought to show a real story that we've read."

"All right. Let's try—" She looked through the box of figures on sticks. "Too many things are missing for any of the fairy stories. There's no wolf for Red Riding Hood, and Cinderella's slipper's gone, and— Oh, I know something! I'll get it!"

Nan put down the box of cardboard figures and dashed up the stairs. She hurried out to the garage and went to a closet, where she had recalled that there were some old cutouts the younger twins had had. Long ago these and several other things had been put in the garage after an outdoor Halloween party.

It was a clear night, so Nan did not bother to turn on the light in the garage. There was one in the closet that she would switch on.

Just as Nan opened the closet door, she heard footsteps outside. At first she thought Bert had followed her, but suddenly a long shadow was cast on the ground just outside. A man was coming slowly around the side of the building.

It was not Mr. Bobbsey; he had gone out. And the shadow was too tall for Sam. It must be a burglar! Maybe the same person who had been there before!

"What shall I do?" thought Nan. "Shall I scream and try to scare him away?"

Nan decided this might not be wise. The man might harm her. There was no chance for her to get out of the garage without being seen. And nothing in the closet behind which she could hide.

Suddenly Nan thought of something. She would disguise herself and try to look like a make-believe figure! She reached up to the closet shelf and felt around until her fingers touched a false face with a wig. It was a scary face with wild hair.

Nan slipped it on, then leaned against the wall as if she were propped up. A second later a flashlight was turned full on her.

To Nan's astonishment the person holding the light gave a loud cry. "Ahoy! It's a ghost!" he wailed, and rushed out of the garage.

Nan pulled off the false face and dashed to the door. The man was just leaping over the back fence. Either he did not know where the gate was, or else he was in too much of a hurry to open it.

Nan had been frightened for a minute. But now she laughed and ran to the house to tell Bert the story.

"That man I scared away said 'Ahoy!'" she told her twin. "I'll bet he's a sailor."

"I'll bet he *was* Matey Foster!" declared Bert. "Tomorrow I'm going down to the docks and try to find him!"

The boy started off early the next morning to do this. He stopped for his friend Charlie Mason, and together they went to the place where the lake and the river met. There was a lot of activity, because a ship was being loaded.

"Gee, that's a really big ship," Bert remarked. "I wonder where it's going."

"To India," replied a workman who was pushing a cart filled with boxes.

At this moment a short, poorly dressed sailor came up to him and said, " 'Ahoy, shipmate! Can you spare a little money so the old sea dog can get something to eat?"

"Where's the sea dog?" whispered Charlie to Bert.

He had spoken louder than he had meant to.

"I'm him!" the sailor answered. "I'm an old salt, an old sea dog, and I'm hungry."

"What ship did you sail on?" Charlie inquired, as the man with the cart pushed off.

"The *Spray* that was sunk off Stony Island."

"Are you Matey Foster?" asked Bert excitedly.

"No. My name's Joe Norton. Joe, the sea dog, they call me. Well, I got to get some money. I'm hungry."

"Please wait a minute," Bert begged. "Tell

me about the *Spray*. Were you on it when it went down?"

The elderly sailor chuckled. "How about payin' to hear my story?" he said. "I can always talk better after I eat."

"What do you mean?" Bert asked him.

"You buy this sea dog's breakfast, and I'll tell you anything you want to know about the *Spray.*"

Bert thought this was a funny way to get a story, but he agreed. He and Charlie and Joe went to a diner across the street. The boys each ordered a glass of milk. Bert said he could spend twenty-five cents for Joe Norton's breakfast, so the man bought oatmeal, rolls, and coffee.

"Well, I tell you," he said to the boys as he ate, "I sailed many a voyage on the *Spray* with Cap'n Dawson."

"Were you on the ship when it went down?" Bert asked

"No, siree." Joe wagged his head. "Good thing, too. Every last one on her went down."

"I thought Matey Foster was saved," said Bert.

"I don't believe he was aboard. That fellow ain't tellin' the truth, any more'n he tells the truth about that model of the *Spray* he says he owns."

"What!" cried Bert. "You know about the model?"

"Sure. Matey Foster claims Cap'n Dawson gave him the model, but the cap'n told me he made it for his son Philip, and wanted him to be sure to have it."

"Where is Philip now?" Bert asked, deciding then and there the rightful owner should have the model.

Joe Norton said he did not know, but he had heard Philip had joined the Navy.

"Guess he likes the water same as his pa did. Some fellow told me he looks like his old man, too—tall and thin."

"You mean someone saw him around here?" Bert asked excitedly.

"Uh-huh."

"He's in Lakeport now?"

"I don't think so."

"Are you sure?"

"Son, I ain't sure o' nuthin'," Joe replied. "Not even where my next meal's comin' from."

Bert thought it was time to leave before the old sailor did any more begging. And evidently he had told all he knew. The boy motioned to

Charlie. They were about to leave, when Joe Norton pointed out the window and said:

"There goes Matey Foster now—with that boy."

As Bert Bobbsey looked, he said, "Gosh!" very loud.

Walking alongside a small, squat man who wore sailors' clothes was Danny Rugg!

CHAPTER X

WAGGO PLAYS DETECTIVE

"YOU'D better wait," Charlie Mason advised
Bert as the boy started out of the diner after
Matey Foster and Danny Rugg.

"Guess you're right," said Bert. "But I'd like
to know what they're doing."

"You've got me. Maybe Danny sold him his
bike," suggested Charlie.

"I'll bet it's more than that," said Bert. "Come
on. It won't hurt to follow them and see where
they're going."

The boys followed the sailor and Danny for
three blocks along the water front. Then Danny
went off. Matey Foster sat down on a bench. Bert
and Charlie strolled up and seated themselves
beside him.

"Ahoy, fellows!" said Foster.

"Good morning," the boys answered, and Bert
added, "You're Matey Foster, aren't you?"

"The same. Everybody knows me, I guess. Only survivor of the *Spray*."

Bert and Charlie looked at each other.

"Listen, lads," the sailor went on, "there's them that says old Matey Foster wasn't on the *Spray* when it went down. Guess I ought to know better'n them!"

He told a horrible story of the sinking. Bert and Charlie listened openmouthed, even though they were not sure how much of the story was true.

"And so here I am, hale and hearty," the sailor finished. "But it was awful, lads, awful!"

"Is it true," Bert asked him, "that you owned a model of the *Spray?*"

"Sure did, son. Had it for years and a mighty nifty little thing she was, too. But she cluttered up my place, so I finally sold her to a second-hand fellow."

"How did you happen to have the ship model?" Bert asked him.

Matey Foster looked a little frightened for a moment, the boy thought. Then the sailor said Captain Dawson had given it to him.

"Why didn't you give it to his son Philip?" Bert wanted to know.

"It seems to me," said Matey Foster, suddenly

getting up from the bench and wagging his finger angrily at Bert Bobbsey, "it seems to me you'd better mind your own business, son. You're a fresh kid. Too smart for your years, I'd say. You'll forget about that ship model if you know what's good for you!"

He walked away quickly. Bert and Charlie stared after him; then Charlie said:

"Matey Foster sure didn't like what you said. I'll bet he knows more'n he's telling."

"You know what I think?" said Bert. "I think that he's afraid somebody'll tell Philip Dawson he stole the ship model."

"Stole it?" Charlie gasped. "Gee whiz, Bert, if it was stolen, you might get in trouble. People who buy things that were stolen sometimes get in trouble."

Bert was worried. He didn't want to get into any trouble because he had bought the model of the *Spray!* He would try hard to find Philip Dawson and give it to him.

"I wish I knew why Danny Rugg was down here with Matey Foster," he said presently. "Let's go see if we can find out."

The two boys spent the rest of the morning looking for Danny, but they did not find him. Charlie said he would like to see the ship model, so they went to the Bobbsey house and climbed the stairs to Bert's bedroom.

"Gee, that's swell!" cried Charlie, upon seeing the *Spray*.

He lifted it down from the highboy where it stood on a bracket, and examined the two masts, the thread ropes, the sails, and all the gadgets on the model. Not an item had been overlooked by the wood carver, Captain Dawson.

"I wish this was mine," Charlie said admiringly.

"Maybe it won't be mine long," Bert sighed.

He set the model back just as Freddie came into the room. When the two older boys left, Freddie wondered why they had been so interested in the little schooner. He climbed onto a chair and took it down from the highboy.

"It *is* nice," he said to himself as he looked at the model. "I wonder if it would sail."

Freddie decided to try the small ship in the bathtub. No one was around to stop him, and he pushed the *Spray* back and forth for twenty minutes. It did not sink.

"Oh, Freddie," said Flossie suddenly, coming in to watch him. She had just arrived home from a toy-collecting trip. "The *Spray's* just like a real ship, isn't it?"

"Sure is," said Freddie, then spoke to Waggo, who had followed Flossie upstairs. "Get down!" he commanded.

The fox terrier had put his paws up on the edge of the tub and was looking at the floating model. Now he reached one paw out trying to touch it.

"Stop!" cried Freddie.

He lifted the ship model out of the water and dried it with a towel. Flossie advised him not to try putting the *Spray* back on the highboy because he might drop it. So her twin laid the ship model on his bed.

Flossie and Freddie started to play tag in the hall, and did not notice that Waggo had jumped up on the bed. The little dog began to dig at a tiny hatch in the deck. Then Dinah called to the children to stop their noise, and they went into Freddie and Bert's room.

"Waggo, what are you doing?" exclaimed Flossie. "Get away from Bert's ship!"

But Waggo did not obey. Something about the model seemed to be worrying him. He sniffed and barked at it. Again he scratched at the tiny deck.

"What do you s'pose he's after?" asked Flossie.

"I don't know," Freddie replied. "Get down, Waggo!" he ordered.

Still Waggo would not obey. Finally he loosened a piece of wood on the deck. It was a hatch cover over an opening into the hold of the little ship.

"Oh, look!" cried Flossie. "Waggo opened up the ship!"

"I wonder what's down in the hole?" Freddie said.

"Maybe a treasure!" ventured Flossie excitedly.

"I'll see," Freddie decided, trying to reach his hand in.

But even his small hand was too big for the opening. Freddie turned the ship upside down and shook it. Suddenly a folded piece of paper dropped out. As Freddie continued to shake the *Spray,* Flossie tried to read the note.

"What's on it?" Freddie asked.

"Just writing," his twin answered. "Funny writing. I can't read it."

Flossie could read print but not handwriting, unless it was very plain. The handwriting on the ship's note was faded and had numbers mixed in with the writing.

"We'll ask Mother to read it when she comes home," the little girl decided.

She laid the note on the bed. Freddie put down the model when he found nothing more was going to fall out of it. A paper they could not read was not much of a treasure after all!

"Come on!" he said in disappointment. "Let's go to the toy shop."

The twins ran off, but Waggo did not follow them. He was still interested in the ship model and the piece of paper. Jumping up on the bed, he nosed the *Spray,* turning it round and round.

Next the little dog took the piece of paper in his mouth and ran downstairs. A little later on he whined at the kitchen door to go out, and Dinah opened it for him.

"Here's a nice beef bone fo' yo'," she chuckled. "And don't yo' bury it in de flower garden!"

It was several hours afterward, when the Bobbsey family gathered for dinner, that Flossie and Freddie told about the note that had fallen out of the ship model. Their parents and the other twins were very much excited to know what it said. Flossie went upstairs to get the note.

"It's gone! The note's gone!" she cried out, running down the stairs.

The others hurried up to the bedroom. The

note was not on the bed. It was not in sight anywhere.

"Oh, dear, this may be a great loss," said Mr.
Bobbsey. "Now, Flossie and Freddie, think
hard. Maybe you put the note somewhere else."

The small twins were sure it had been left on
the bed. And no one had been in the room besides themselves.

"No one except Waggo," said Flossie.

Bert brought the little dog into the house,
tapped the ship model on the bed, and said:

"Find the paper, Waggo! Find the paper you
took away!"

But Waggo just stood still, wagged his tail
hard, and acted as if he were being asked to play
a game. At last the Bobbseys gave up trying to
make him understand.

"If Waggo took the note, we'll find it!" declared Bert. "Let's look everywhere."

The hunt started.

CHAPTER XI

A MERRY HUNT

IN THE midst of the hunt for the lost paper, Dinah called upstairs. She wanted to know when the family was going to eat.

"De roast chicken's gettin' all dried up. De peas are mush. And de glasses o' milk are goin' to turn sour any minute," she complained.

Mrs. Bobbsey smiled at Dinah's worries, but said the family had better get down to the table at once! As soon as the meal was over, the search for the missing paper started again.

The younger twins and their mother searched the second floor. Mr. Bobbsey hunted outdoors. Bert and Nan went over every inch of the first floor. They even looked under the edges of the rugs.

"That note's gone for good," sighed Nan, when the entire family reported failure. "And it probably was an important message."

Flossie and Freddie felt sorry that they had not taken better care of it. The little twins had been sure the note would be found, and had not worried until now.

"Maybe Waggo swallowed it!" said Flossie.

"No," said Freddie. "Only goats eat paper. And he's not a goat."

The others did not think Waggo had eaten the paper. They were sure he had not even torn it, because if so, they would have found the bits.

"I'll bet that note told the secret about the real *Spray*," declared Bert. "Now maybe we'll never know what it was."

Mr. and Mrs. Bobbsey were more hopeful that the mystery would be solved. But for the time being everyone gave up trying to figure it out.

The following morning something new came up that took the minds of the older twins off the note. Uncle Linn Smith said he had received an order for merry-go-round animals.

"That's a big play toy." Nan laughed. "What would a child want with such things?"

"This is not for a small child," Uncle Linn replied. "A grown-up child wants them." Then, his eyes twinkling, he said:

"On a merry-go-round ride young and old
Music! Laughter! What a din!
As someone catches the ring of brass,
Even the wooden animals grin."

Nan and Bert grinned, too. Then Uncle Linn told them that a man whose business it was to dress store windows wanted to use the merry-go-round animals for decorations.

"I don't usually go in for this sort of thing," said the toy mender, "but the man will pay well for the animals. I thought I'd give the money to Ruthie Watson. It would help pay for the operation Dr. Benson said she ought to have."

"Oh!" said Nan. "I thought the doctor was going to arrange that for her."

"He will do all he can," replied Uncle Linn. "But, of course, there will be lots of other expenses besides the operation itself. Well, now, about the animals. My sister Sallie said someone told her a farmer over in Daleville bought an old broken-down merry-go-round at an auction. Maybe he'll sell the animals."

"Maybe Sam could take us there in one of Dad's trucks," Bert offered. "I'll phone him."

When Mr. Bobbsey heard the request, he

said he would be glad to help out. Sam had to deliver some lumber in Daleville, and the twins could go along.

"After Sam delivers the orders, he can drive you wherever you want to go," Bert's father told him. "Come right down."

Bert reported this to Uncle Linn and asked the name of the farmer who had the old merry-go-round.

"That's the trouble," the toy mender answered. "I don't know. And the woman who told Aunt Sallie about it has moved to Canada."

"Then we'll ask people in Daleville," said Bert. "Somebody will know."

Sam had the truck loaded by the time Bert and Nan got to the yard.

"All aboard!" called the genial colored man. "We're all ready to sail." He had worked on a lumber schooner before being hired by Mr. Bobbsey. "Get right up into de cabin!" and Sam indicated the high, wide seat of the truck.

Perched up there, Nan and Bert had a good chance to see the lovely, rolling country around Lakeport, because Sam did not drive very fast. When they reached Daleville, he announced he would be some time delivering the lumber.

"If yo' all wants to go lookin' fo' secondhand toys, yo'll have plenty ob time," Sam announced.

"That's fine," said Nan.

"And we can ask who owns the merry-go-round animals," her twin added.

The children called at several homes in the little town. When they told their errand, they were given a Punch-and-Judy show and two sleds, but no one knew where the merry-go-round animals might be.

"I guess we'll just have to go from door to door and ask," sighed Nan as the twins met Sam.

"Take yo' time," said the colored man.

They stopped at several farmhouses but had no luck. The twins had just concluded that Aunt Sallie Pry must have been mistaken and they might as well go home, when Bert pointed out a large, well-kept farm just ahead. In the yard stood a white wooden horse hitched to a sleigh!

"I'll bet this is the place where the merry-go-round animals are," he said excitedly.

Sam drove into the lane, and the twins hopped out. Nan asked a woman who came to the door if she had any merry-go-round animals. The woman looked very much surprised, then smiled, and said:

"I'm afraid not. I suppose you thought the

one attached to the sleigh came from a merry-
go-round, but I don't think so. You see, we've
lived here only a month. The owner died and
we bought the place furnished. We hardly know
what's in it ourselves, we've been so busy working, but I've never seen any other wooden animals."

The Bobbseys told her about their collecting
secondhand toys, mending them, and sending
them to children who had few of their own.

"Well, I can help you out there," the woman
said. "The former owner of this place left a
pile of old toys. You're welcome to all you want.
They're in a storeroom in the barn. I'll show
you."

Nan and Bert followed her to the barn, which
was a large one.

"The storeroom is up those stairs," she said,
pointing. "You can go up by yourselves. I'm not
good at climbing."

Nan and Bert went up the stairs, which were
covered with wisps of hay and straw. There were
no horses in the barn, the twins learned, because
the new owner used a tractor and other ma-
chinery for his work.

The storeroom was dimly lighted by a window. By the little sunshine which filtered feebly

through the dusty panes, Nan and Bert saw several toys they knew would delight Uncle Linn.

"Oh, this is wonderful!" Nan exulted.

"Quite a find," said Bert. He began to pick up old jumping jacks and boxes of blocks.

Nan wandered into a far corner, not minding the dust and cobwebs. Suddenly she cried out:

"Oh, Bert!"

"What is it?" he asked.

"Come here and look!" Nan exclaimed.

"Here's a whole bunch of good stuff!"

"What kind?"

"A hobbyhorse, and the cutest little milk wagon, and— Oh!"

Nan's excited remarks suddenly ended in a frightened cry. Then her cry faded. Bert heard a loud thud!

CHAPTER XII

THE STRANGE LOAD

BERT jumped toward the dark corner from which Nan had so suddenly vanished.

"Where are you?" he called.

"Down here," answered Nan's distant voice. "I fell down a hay chute."

"Are you hurt?" questioned Bert.

"Not much. I'm in a horse stall."

"I'll come down and help you. Watch out!"

"Wait till I get out of the way," Nan warned him. "I fell on something hard. I'll put some more hay for you to land on." Then she cried, "Oh, Bert, there's an elephant here, and a camel, and a lion, and—"

"Nan, are you all right?" Bert shouted down in alarm.

"Of course I'm all right," Nan replied.

"I thought maybe you landed on your head and—"

"You thought maybe I was seeing things?"

Nan laughed. "I'm not. Bert, the merry-go-round animals are here!"

"Honest? Hold everything! I'm coming down!"

Bert slid down the fodder chute and landed in a pile of hay. He was in the middle of a large box stall from which the manger had been removed.

"Look!" cried Nan, pointing under a pile of hay along one wall.

Stacked in a row were several large, gaily painted animals; three horses, two elephants, a camel, a lion, and a fierce-looking tiger.

"They're from a merry-go-round all right," said Bert. "Gee, I'm glad we found them."

"Do you think the farmer and his wife will sell these?" asked Nan.

"If they didn't even know they were here, I guess they won't care about them," Bert answered.

"Let's ask the lady."

"How do we get out of here?" Nan worried. "I hope we don't have to go up that chute! I hurt my ankle a little."

"Can you walk all right?"

"Oh, sure, I just bruised it."

Bert looked around. "There's a door," he said, and indicated one on the other side of the box stall, half hidden by the piles of hay.

He and Nan tugged at the door and got out. Then they found the farmer's wife. She laughed when they told her of the unexpected discovery.

"Would you sell the wooden animals?" Bert asked her.

"Why, I guess so," she replied. "I'll ask my husband how he feels about it. Here he comes now."

The farmer chugged into the barnyard on his tractor. His wife and the Bobbsey twins went to meet him, and told their story. The man grinned broadly.

"Imagine that, Sara! All those wild animals in our barn and we didn't know it!"

When the farmer heard that they would be used to help lame little Ruthie Watson, he said he would be glad to give them to Uncle Linn.

"Gee, that's swell," said Bert.

"Thank you very much," Nan said, smiling. "If you'll let us take the wooden animals right now, we can put them on the truck."

"Sure," said the farmer.

Nan ran to the house to tell Sam.

"Ready to go?" he asked.

"Yes," was the answer. "But first we have to collect a lion and a tiger and a camel and an elephant."

Sam jumped in the seat. "Now, Miss Nan—" he said.

"What's the matter?" she asked.

"'Scuse me!" gasped Sam. "I'll do most anything t' help, but I'm not goin' t' mess with lions or tigers! No, sir!"

"They're only wooden." Nan laughed. "They're the merry-go-round animals we've been looking for."

"Oh!" said Sam, relieved, and laughed. "Dat's different."

He drove down to the barn and helped load the wooden animals onto the truck. They were much heavier than anyone had suspected. Sam chuckled.

"If dese wild animules weren't so tame, I sure could believe dey *were* alive!" he remarked. "I'se carried all sorts o' things in my truck but never nothin' like this."

All the way back to the toy shop people on the street stared at the strange load. Uncle Linn beamed when he saw it.

"Fine! Fine!" he praised the twins. "You

children are good detectives. I didn't really expect you to find these animals."

The wooden figures were set in a corner of the toy shop. Then the other toys the children had collected were brought in. Uncle Linn thought the Punch-and-Judy show was a very good one, even though Punch's dog Toby was missing.

"We'll have to find a dog somewhere," he said.

"I'll help you," offered Flossie Bobbsey, who came into the toy mender's barn at that very second.

Freddie was right behind her. The small twins were excited at seeing the things their brother and sister had brought. At once they forgot why they had come to the shop—which was to tell Nan and Bert to hurry home to lunch —and began to play merry-go-round with the wooden animals.

Bert started work on the Punch-and-Judy stage. Nan tried to fix up Judy's white cap and apron, which were torn. Uncle Linn was doing the best he could with one hand to put Punch's peaked cap and neck ruff into shape. As the toy mender looked at the little figure's birdlike features, large nose, and the humps in front and in back of his chest, he chuckled. Then he said aloud:

"Did you ever hear of a man being a hundred years old before he got married?"

"No. Did you?" laughed Nan.

"Yes," said Uncle Linn. "It was Mr. Punch here."

"What do you mean?" asked Bert, puzzled.

"It's a fact," the toy mender went on. "Mr. Punch and his dog appeared in shows in England way back in 1688. But it wasn't until a hundred years later that someone got the idea of putting a Mrs. Punch in the show for Mr. Punch to tease."

"Like this," said Bert.

He gave a good imitation of the voice of Mr. Punch as he had heard it in shows, and Nan pretended to be his wife. She began to scold him for being late to dinner. When Flossie and Freddie heard this, they got down from the wooden animals at once.

"Oh, we were s'posed to tell you to come right home to lunch," Flossie said in dismay. The twins hurried off to one of Dinah's delicious sausage-and-waffle lunches.

In the afternoon only Bert and Nan returned to the shop. Freddie went to Teddy Blake's, and Flossie said she and Susie Larker had a special errand to do. The little girl was very mysterious about it.

Late that day Bert and Nan left for an overnight party at the lake cabin of a boy who was in their class at school. They stayed all the next day, too, swimming and having beach picnics.

"Did you have fun?" Flossie asked them two mornings later, as the four twins set off for the toy shop.

"You bet," Bert answered. "But one of my steak sandwiches fell in the fire and burned up."

"And I jabbed a hole in my rubber duck," said Nan, laughing.

As the children approached Uncle Linn's barn, they saw a large black dog tied to the handle of the door.

"Whose dog is that?" Bert asked.

Before anyone could answer, the animal made a leap, broke the rope by which he was tied, and rushed straight for Flossie!

CHAPTER XIII

GONE!

NAN screamed, and leaped toward her sister. Bert picked up a stick and started for the big black dog, which was now close to Flossie.

"Run, Flossie!" cried Freddie.

"Why should I run?" asked the little girl calmly. "This is my new dog. Don't hit him!"

"*Your* dog?" gasped the other twins.

"Sure. Hello, Watch," said Flossie, patting the dog. "He likes me."

It was evident the new dog did like her. He leaped playfully about Flossie and tried to lick her face in a friendly way.

"Down, Watch, down!" Flossie ordered him.

"Well, what do you know about that?" Bert grinned, as the dog obeyed the little girl.

Freddie began to play with Watch. "He's a swell dog," said the boy. "Can he do tricks?"

"I don't know," his twin answered.

"Where'd you get him?" asked Nan.

"A lady gave him to me," Flossie said. "Susie and I went hunting for toys and dogs the other day. None of the other people wanted to give their dogs away. But Mrs. Thompson didn't mind."

"How did Mrs. Thompson happen to give you the dog?" Bert wanted to know.

"I asked her," answered Flossie, as she patted her new pet. "I heard Uncle Linn say he wanted a dog, and I told him I'd hunt for one. When I went to Mrs. Thompson's house, Watch was tied to her porch. Susie and I played with him, and we liked him. I said could I have him, and Mrs. Thompson said yes. Then she said her husband would leave Watch here when he went to work today, and here he is."

Bert and Nan were puzzled. They could not remember Uncle Linn having said he wanted a dog. The toy mender came out of his house just then, and he, too, was puzzled.

"But you did say you'd have to find a dog," Flossie insisted.

Suddenly Uncle Linn, Bert, and Nan began to laugh. They had wanted to find a new dog for Mr. Punch, because Toby was missing from the Punch-and-Judy show.

"We meant a toy dog," Nan explained to her sister.

Flossie was sad. She was afraid she would have to take Watch back.

"Can't I please keep him?" she begged.

Uncle Linn looked at Watch, who seemed very content.

"Maybe we should have a watchdog for the toy shop," he said. "Last night when I came out here to look things over, I saw a sailor sneaking away from the barn. It was locked, but I had an idea he might have been planning to break in."

"To steal toys?" gasped Flossie. "What a mean man!"

Bert suspected the sailor might have been Matey Foster. Perhaps he thought the ship model of the *Spray* was in the toy shop and had come to steal it.

"What did he look like?" the boy asked Uncle Linn.

"I couldn't see his face," the toy mender answered. "He ran off too fast. He seemed short and fat, though."

"It must have been Matey Foster!" exclaimed Bert. "Well, we'd better keep Watch here to guard this place."

The dog seemed happy to stay. He did not

attempt to run back to his former home. Whenever customers came to Mr. Hewson's upstairs
toy shop, he barked a friendly greeting.

"He's a 'nouncer dog," said Flossie, happy
that he was useful and could announce strangers
with his barking.

Uncle Linn told the children he thought they
should pack some of the toys—at least, he and
the older twins should. The shop was fairly
bursting with toys. There really was no room for
more to be brought in.

"Those boxes you carried from the upstairs toy
store are still in the cellar of my house," said the
toy mender. "Suppose you children bring several of them here, and we'll fill them with toys
that are ready to be sent away."

Freddie and Flossie insisted upon helping, so
they were given the job of sorting the boxes. The
younger twins were told to bring only the stur-
diest ones to the barn.

In the meantime Bert and Nan, under Uncle
Linn's direction, picked out a variety of toys. One
by one the cartons were filled, addressed, and set
in the driveway. Then Bert telephoned to the
express company for a man to call for the boxes.

The three of them were so busy that they did
not notice the little twins. Flossie and Freddie

had finished their job, and were playing with Watch.

"I think I'll get Waggo, so we'll each have a dog," suggested Freddie.

He ran home and got the fox terrier. Waggo and Watch enjoyed playing with the children in Uncle Linn's big yard.

"Oh, here comes the expressman," said Flossie after a while, as a truck came into the driveway. "He's going to take the boxes of toys."

Watch growled and Waggo began to bark.

"We'd better tie the dogs up," advised Freddie.

He fixed the broken rope and tied the big black dog to a clothes post. Flossie could not find anything with which to fasten Waggo. Spying an empty crate near the driveway, she put the little fox terrier inside it, and fastened the lid.

"I'll let you out soon as the 'spressman's gone," she said. "Be a good dog."

Waggo liked to play games, and he thought this was some kind of game. So he did not even bark.

The little twins forgot all about him, because there was so much excitement in the barn. Even before the expressman loaded the boxes onto the truck, the children were called up-stairs. Mr. Hewson, who had the second-floor toy shop, asked if they would help him. The expressman had brought him several packages, and his clerk was not at the store to help open them.

"There are bound to be some things broken," Mr. Hewson said. "And you may as well take them downstairs with you right away. I'm certainly cramped for room here."

"When will your regular toy store be fixed up?" Freddie asked him, as he started to open a large carton.

"Not for a while," Mr. Hewson replied. "The fire was pretty bad. Well, here's something you can have for *your* toy shop," he said, holding up a little chair from which all the legs had been broken off. "It's a musical chair. Sit on it, Flossie."

The little girl seated herself on the small, up-holstered armchair. At once it began to play "Three Blind Mice." Flossie was so surprised she jumped up. The music stopped. Then she laughed and sat down again.

"See how they run," the musical chair went on, and finished the tune.

"Oh, isn't that cute?" said Nan.

"That's not all," said Mr. Hewson, taking something else out of the carton. "These little wooden dolls go on the arms of the chair."

Flossie got up while Mr. Hewson fastened the figures into little holes on the arms. This time when she sat down another tune began to play. It was "Rings on My Fingers, Bells on My Toes." The little wooden men and women spun around, and moved their arms and legs in time to the music, or so it seemed.

"It's be—yootiful!" cried Flossie. "Do you really mean we can have it?"

"The chair can't be sold without legs," said Mr. Hewson. "The toy is already a secondhand one. Or should I say a no-leg one?" he laughed.

The children thanked him. Bert said he would carry the chair downstairs. Flossie and Freddie ran ahead of him. As they reached the first floor, Watch whined outside.

"Oh, he wants to get loose," said Freddie. "I'll untie him."

Flossie suddenly remembered poor Waggo shut up in the crate. She rushed to the yard to let him out.

"Why, where is he?" Flossie said aloud, because the crate was not where she had left it.

Deciding the expressman must have moved

it, she looked all around. The crate was not in sight.

"I guess someone let Waggo out and he ran home," Flossie decided.

The little girl thought no more about it until that evening. Then she learned that Waggo had not come home. Flossie became worried. Maybe the Bobbsey pet was still in the crate somewhere.

Nan and Bert knew nothing about the dog. In alarm the twins went over to Uncle Linn's house. The toy mender said he had not seen Waggo. Before locking the barn and tying the new dog up, he had looked around the place thoroughly.

"Your dog wasn't here," he said. Suddenly a strange look came over his face. "Where did you last see him?" he asked quickly.

"I shut him up in a crate," Flossie replied. "When I came back for him, he was gone."

"Crate, eh?" said Uncle Linn. "Then I guess I know where Waggo is."

"Where?" cried the twins together.

"On a train bound for Chicago!" Uncle Linn replied.

CHAPTER XIV

LOOKING FOR TREASURE

THE Bobbsey twins stared at Uncle Linn Smith. What did he mean?

"Waggo's on a train?" gasped Nan. "Going to Chicago? But how? Who—?"

"It's only a guess, of course," said Uncle Linn. "But this is the way I figure it. My sister Sallie planned to send a fern to a cousin of ours in Chicago. I fixed up a crate for it, and painted the name and address on it. But she never sent the fern. Flossie must have put Waggo in the crate. I believe the expressman took him away."

"Maybe he's in the express office downtown," said Bert hopefully. "Let's go find out."

"I'm sure you won't find Waggo there." Uncle Linn shook his head. "Live animals and plants are always shipped as soon as they are received by the express company."

"Oh, dear," wailed Flossie. "What'll we do?

114

Poor Waggo won't have any dinner. And—"
She started to cry.

Uncle Linn patted the little girl on the shoulder. "Don't worry, Flossie," he said. "The men in the baggage cars on trains always take good care of dogs. They feed them, and even let them out for a run once in a while."

"But Waggo won't know where he is, and he won't have any home," Freddie spoke up. The little boy was ready to cry too.

"I'll see to that," said Uncle Linn. "First I'll make sure the expressman did take Waggo by mistake. Then, if he did, I'll telegraph my cousin to take care of the dog and ship him back at once."

The toy mender knew the express company driver well. He came to the toy shop about once a week to pick up packages. Uncle Linn telephoned his house, while the Bobbseys stood by, listening. They were terribly excited. Finally Uncle Linn hung up and smiled.

"Waggo is on a train bound for Chicago, all right," he said. "But don't worry about him. By this time he's had his supper and is probably sound asleep in the baggage car."

It was hard for the twins not to worry about their pet. They hoped people would be kind to him and feed him the proper food. That night Flossie dreamed Waggo got loose in the train, woke everybody up with his barking, and was taken away by a policeman.

By the next evening she felt better, however. Uncle Linn's cousin in Chicago had telegraphed to say she had Waggo and would ship him right back.

"He is a dear little dog, and I hate to part with him," she had wired. "Tell the children he has done several tricks. I am sure he is happy."

"Oh, goody, goody!" cried Flossie. "Waggo is safe!"

She danced around the floor and then dashed out to the kennel to tell old Snap that his playmate was all right.

"Waggo's an awful long way from here," she told Snap, "but he'll be home soon." Flossie was a little annoyed that Snap was not more interested.

It was hard for the children to settle down to work, while waiting for the fox terrier to return. Uncle Linn said he was going to declare the following day a holiday.

"No work tomorrow," he announced. "You children have stuck very close to the shop, and done a wonderful job. You must have other things you'd like to do—go riding or see a ball game, for instance."

Bert immediately knew what he wanted to do; go to Stony Island and find out more about the sunken *Spray*. The piece of paper from the ship model which might have supplied the answer to the mystery had not been found. If the mystery were ever to be solved, it would have to be solved some other way.

"I think I'll ask Charlie Mason to go out to the island with me," he decided, and dropped by Charlie's house on the way home.

"Sure," his friend said at once. "Let's go early. We can fish, and swim, and—"

"And hunt for a treasure," added Bert, grinning.

The next morning the two boys met at a dock and rented a rowboat. Standing not far away was Danny Rugg. He was hoping to see Matey Foster, who usually wandered along the water front early in the morning.

"Hope you catch some fish, boys," said the dockman to Bert and Charlie, as they pulled away. "I see you've got a pail with you."

"Wish us luck about a treasure, too," laughed Bert, who was at the oars.

Danny was curious. Where were the boys going? He wished Matey Foster would come. Then they could follow and see what was going on. Danny was still mad at Bert because he had not sold him the ship model, and he felt Bert was responsible for his punishment in regard to the bicycle.

"I'll get square yet," Danny determined. "As soon as Matey comes—here he comes now!"

In the meantime, Bert and Charlie had headed out from shore. Stony Island was about a mile away, in the middle of the river. When they got near it, Charlie lifted up the pail he had brought.

"You want to start fishing now?" Bert asked.

Charlie explained that this was a spyglass pail; not a pail for fish, although any fish they might catch could be put into it later.

"Dad used this one time when he was trying to locate a suitcase that had dropped overboard," Charlie explained. "He put the glass in."

Mr. Mason had knocked the bottom out of an old wooden pail and had cemented in a heavy pane of glass, making it watertight with putty. By pushing the glass end down into the water, and thrusting his head into the open pail, he had been able to get a dim view of the depths of the river.

Bert let the rowboat drift and Charlie looked

over the side. He peered intently through the glass, but there was no sign of a wreck here.

"Let's go all the way around the island and look," Bert suggested.

Charlie took the oars, while Bert thrust his head into the glass-bottomed pail. Suddenly he cried out:

"I see something!" His own voice nearly deafened him in the small space. Laughing, he pulled his head out and said excitedly, "I think the *Spray's* down below here. I can just make out something darker than the water. Let's dive in and see what's doing."

The boys wore swimming trunks under their clothes. After pulling the rowboat up on shore, they peeled off their shirts and trousers, and dived in. Both of the boys were excellent swimmers.

They swam out a hundred yards from shore, and then dived down. Below them lay what was left of the wrecked schooner *Spray*. If the boys had been able to reach her, they would have seen that her masts and ropes were gone, and most of the deck. But the metal hull was still there.

"Wow!" gasped Bert, coming to the surface a moment after Charlie had. "That's—sure—far —down!"

"I'll—say," panted Charlie. "Guess—we can't —do much—exploring."

The boys turned over on their backs and rested on the water before swimming to shore. Then, when they reached it, they lay down a little while to rest and dry off.

"What kind of treasure do you think is in the *Spray?*" Charlie asked presently.

"Money, probably," Bert answered. "People say Captain Dawson never kept his money in banks."

"If the money was in bills, they aren't much good by this time," Charlie remarked.

"Unless they were in a watertight box."

"That's right." Charlie was enthusiastic for a minute, then he added, "I don't see why they haven't sent a diver down to hunt for it."

"Uncle Linn said it would cost a lot of money," Bert answered. "I guess nobody would want to do it unless he was sure there really is a treasure down there. Gee," he added after a moment, "I wish Freddie and Flossie hadn't lost that paper in the ship model."

"That sure was hard luck," said Charlie. "But maybe it'll turn up. Say, do you suppose Waggo buried the paper like he does bones?"

"You might be right," Bert said, taking hope. "Let's go to my house and start looking."

"Okay."

The boys started up the shore of the little island. After they had walked a few minutes, Charlie asked:

"Where'd we leave our boat? I thought it was here."

Bert gazed about him. Then he walked slowly around the spot.

"That's funny," he said.

The boys stared along the beach in both directions, but there was no sign of the rowboat.

"Gee whiz, Charlie," Bert cried at last, "our boat's gone!"

"What do you mean?" Charlie asked. "Didn't you pull it up on shore far enough?"

"Sure I did. Look! Here are the tracks!"

The boys stared at each other. Someone had taken their boat while they were in swimming!

CHAPTER XV

FREDDIE'S MISTAKE

BERT and Charlie flopped to the ground.

"Gee, what dopes we turned out to be!" said Charlie in disgust. "Now how are we going to get home? We can't swim to Lakeport."

Bert was furious to think someone had taken their boat and their clothes, and said so. But presently he relaxed and tried to figure out what to do.

"I feel just like Robinson Crusoe," he groaned.

"Yeh, and I suppose I'm your man Friday." Charlie grinned. "Well, how'd you like some tree leaves and grass for lunch?"

The two boys were very hungry after their strenuous swim. The more they thought about food, the hungrier they got.

"Say," said Bert, "there might be somebody else on this island. We didn't go all the way around it. Maybe someone's on the other side with a boat and will give us a ride to Lakeport!"

"Sure, there might be a fisherman," said Charlie.

The boys started a tour of the island. It did not take long, for the place was small. But there was no one else on the island.

"If a boat passes us on the river, we'll shout," Bert suggested.

But no boat came along. The boys got hungrier by the minute.

"Gee," said Charlie a little later, "this is fierce. What say we try swimming ashore?"

"And if we don't make it?" asked Bert. "No, Charlie, that's out. Somebody's bound to come— Hey!" he cried suddenly. "Hey!"

In the distance was a man in a rowboat. Both boys yelled at the top of their lungs, and finally the man heard them. As he neared the island they saw that he was dressed in sailors' clothes.

"Joe Norton!" Bert called to him.

"What's the matter?" the man asked. "Ye two shipwrecked?"

Bert told him what had happened.

"Did you see anyone on the river with an extra rowboat?" he asked.

"Sure did," Joe replied. "Feller about your age had one in tow."

"Who was he?" Bert asked excitedly.

"I dunno. Could 'a' been the one I showed you was with Matey Foster that day. Remember?"

Danny Rugg!

"Say, do you want me to find out?" asked Joe.

"No, thanks," said Bert. He was afraid Joe might ask for another meal in payment for the information! "Say, you going back to town?" he asked.

"I might consider it," Joe chuckled, and hesitated. Was he going to request payment for the ride? However, he merely said, "Well, hop aboard, you two landlubbers."

The boys waded out and climbed in. All the way back to Lakeport they kept their eyes open for the missing boat. To their amazement, the man at the rental dock said he had found it there half an hour before. Their clothes and the glass-bottomed bucket were in it.

"But I didn't see who brought the rowboat in," the man told them. "You say someone took it?"

Bert nodded. "Did a boy named Danny Rugg rent a boat from you today?"

"No."

"Did Matey Foster?"

"Yes, he did."

Bert said no more. He wondered if **Danny** had got the sailor to rent a boat for him.

"I'd like to bet Danny saw us, Charlie, and heard me talking about the treasure," Bert told his friend as the two boys separated to go to their own homes.

"I'll try to find out," Charlie promised, as he went off.

Just after Bert reached home, Waggo arrived. He was sitting on the front seat beside the expressman, as the man drove up in his truck.

"Waggo!" exclaimed Flossie, who was the first one to see the dog. "My precious Waggo!"

She hugged her pet until he squirmed away from her. Each of the twins took turns welcoming Waggo home.

"I wish he could talk and tell us about his trip," sighed Flossie.

"And I wish he could tell us where that missing paper is," said Bert.

But Waggo did not seem interested in anything at the moment but a large bowl of meat and dog biscuits which Dinah had fixed for him.

"Dey must 'a' starved yo', sho' 'nough," she chuckled. "My, such gobblin'!"

"Maybe Waggo did eat that piece of paper," Bert said gloomily.

Then he remembered Charlie's suggestion that Waggo might have buried the note as he did his favorite bones. Bert sprang up excitedly.

"Maybe, if I make Waggo sniff the ship model again," he exclaimed, "he'll remember the note and show me where he buried it."

Bert dashed upstairs to the room he shared with Freddie. Then, as he started over to the highboy where he kept the ship model, his mouth fell open in amazement.

The ship model was gone!

After looking around the room and not seeing it anywhere else, Bert dashed downstairs to ask Dinah if she knew where the *Spray* was.

"Why, no, Bert," she said. "I done dusted it off not two hours ago, and it sure was in yo' room then."

Bewildered, she and Bert went into the yard to ask Flossie and Freddie, who were watching a squirrel crack nuts, if they knew anything about it.

"Sure I do," Freddie answered. "The man who took it said Mr. Lenter would give you the money."

"What man? What do you mean?" Bert asked in alarm.

"The one the captain's son sent from the store."

"Freddie, *please!*" cried Bert.

Flossie helped her twin tell the story. A man who said he worked for Mr. Lenter had come to the house while she and Freddie were playing in the front yard. He told them Philip Dawson had stopped in Mr. Lenter's shop and found out Bert had the model. So Mr. Lenter had sent his clerk to get it.

"The man asked me to give it to him, so I did," said Freddie. "That was all right, wasn't it, Bert?"

"Sure," Bert answered kindly.

Still, he was puzzled. Why hadn't Mr. Lenter merely telephoned Bert to bring the model down himself? And why hadn't he sent the two dollars to the house, instead of asking Bert to come and get it?

"Now don't yo' fret about it, Bert," Dinah said wisely. "Yo' just go in an' have yo' lunch, and then afterward go see Mr. Lenter an' get everythin' straightened out."

"I guess you're right, Dinah," Bert said, sighing. "I'm sure hungry."

While Bert ate the generous luncheon that Dinah had saved for him, Freddie watched his brother anxiously. He hated to see Bert upset and felt that in some way he was to blame. Bert noticed this, and when he finished eating, said to Freddie:

"How about it? Want to go over to Mr. Lenter's shop with me?"

Freddie's eyes lighted up. Bert wasn't annoyed with him after all!

"Sure I would, Bert," he replied eagerly.

The two Bobbseys started off for Jacob Lenter's secondhand shop. When they reached it, Bert saw the owner working at a desk in the back. He and Freddie went up to him.

"Hello, boys," he said. "What can I do for you today?"

"I came for the money," Bert replied. "I'm glad Mr. Dawson got the ship model, but I'm sure sorry I couldn't keep it myself."

Mr. Lenter frowned. "What's this you say?"

Bert told his story. When he finished, a worried look came over Mr. Lenter's face.

"Bert," he said, "I didn't send a clerk to get the *Spray* from you. And I haven't seen Captain Dawson's son since he was a boy. In fact, I don't know a thing about what you've told me."

Bert and Freddie stared at each other in dismay. This time the ship model *had* been stolen!

CHAPTER XVI

NAN'S DISCOVERY

JACOB LENTER was as alarmed over the theft of the ship model as the Bobbsey boys.

"What did the man who came to the house look like?" he asked Freddie.

Freddie was on the verge of tears. He knew now he had done something dreadful.

"I—I don't remember much about him," he answered. " 'Cept he was short, and kind of fat."

"Did he have on sailors' clothes?" Bert asked quickly, suspecting Matey Foster at once.

"No," Freddie said. "Regular clothes. I wasn't going to give him the ship model," Freddie added. "I told him you weren't home yet, Bert. But when I showed it to him, he just took it, and said for you to get the money from Mr. Lenter."

"Maybe it's just someone playing a joke on you," suggested Mr. Lenter.

"I'm sure it's no joke," Bert said soberly.

129

"Someone has been after the *Spray* right along, and now he's finally got it."

He explained why he thought so. Mysterious persons had been surprised both in the Bobbseys' garage and at Uncle Linn's toy shop.

"I thought at first it was Danny Rugg," Bert went on, "then a sailor came. But the man who took the model wasn't a sailor. I can't figure it out."

"It's a mystery, all right," Mr. Lenter agreed. "If the model isn't returned to you soon, let me know and I'll report it to the police."

Bert and Freddie said good-bye and left the shop. Freddie, still blaming himself, said:

"Maybe Danny knows who took the model. Why don't you ask him, Bert?"

"I will," Bert returned grimly.

The two boys turned down the street on which Danny Rugg lived. As it happened, Danny was standing on the lawn in front of his house when they came along. Bert decided to be cautious about what he said, in case Danny was not guilty.

"So you're still interested in the ship model, eh?" he asked.

Danny eyed Bert suspiciously. "Maybe I am. Maybe I'm not. Why? Did you break it? I wouldn't buy an old broken ship."

"No, I didn't break it," Bert returned, watching Danny carefully. "I just wondered if you still wanted it."

"Well, I don't," Danny snapped. "I've got to save all my money now for something else." He turned away abruptly and went up the steps into his house. Bert stared after him with a puzzled frown.

"Do you think Danny Rugg has the model already, Bert?" Freddie asked eagerly.

Bert shrugged. "Search me," he returned. "But I think this time maybe he's telling the truth. Probably he's saving up for a new bicycle."

"Then who do you think's got the model?" Freddie started to worry all over again. Perhaps the little ship never would turn up.

"I think," said Bert, "Matey Foster came in civvies and took the *Spray*."

"Honest?" Freddie's eyes opened wide. "And what are civvies? He was walking."

Bert laughed. "Civvies is short for civilian clothes. That's what they call the clothes most men wear," Bert explained. "Not uniforms like soldiers or sailors wear."

"The man's clothes were too big for him," Freddie said.

"Matey probably borrowed them from somebody," declared Bert. "I'm going to find him.
It's too late to go down to the docks now, but let's
go tomorrow and hunt for him. Perhaps you'll
recognize him."

Early the next morning the two Bobbsey boys
set out for the docks. Flossie stayed home to play
with Waggo, and Nan planned to ride to the next
town on her bicycle to pick up some toys. Mrs.
Bobbsey had been told about them.

"They're small enough to go in the basket
on your bicycle," she said to Nan.

On the way, Nan stopped at Ruthie Watson's
house to learn how the little lame girl was getting
along.

"When are you going to New York to see the
surgeon, Ruthie?" Nan inquired.

Ruthie hung her head. "We haven't enough
money," she said. "Not even with the money
from the merry-go-round animals. Anyway, the
doctor can't see me for a while yet."

"Oh, I'm terribly sorry," said Nan kindly. "I
wish there were some way I could help."

All the way to the next town she kept worrying about Ruthie. Something would have to be
done to raise the money for the little girl's operation!

"I'll think of something," Nan determined. "Maybe we could run a show and get lots of people to come to it, and give all the money to Ruthie!"

When Nan reached her destination, Mrs. Hatch, who had the toys, was not there. But she had left word that Nan was to wait.

It was late when Mrs. Hatch returned and brought out the various toys she wanted to give away. Most of them were miniatures. Nan was fascinated by the little objects.

"Oh, this violin is only an inch long, and it's perfect!" she exclaimed. "But this toy doesn't need mending," the girl said. "We're looking only for broken toys."

Mrs. Hatch smiled. "This one is the only piece in my set of miniature toys that isn't broken," she said. "So you may as well take them all along."

She handed Nan a wee grand piano with the lid gone; a bed that had no back; a bookcase whose shelves were missing. Tables, chairs, a couch—all needed mending. By the time Nan packed them carefully in the basket of her bicycle, it was nearly full.

"Oh, this is wonderful!" she exclaimed.

"I have one more thing I'd like to give you, Nan," said Mrs. Hatch, "but it's not small.

Maybe you can lay it across the top of the basket."

She went off for a minute and came back with a toy xylophone.

"I used to play this when I was a child," she said, picking up the little wooden hammer.

She played part of a tune on the metal bars, and then stopped suddenly.

"There are two pieces of metal missing," she said. "The notes F and G. You can't play it very well without them."

"I guess not," said Nan. "But I think my twin brother Bert or Uncle Linn can put in new pieces."

"They must be in scale with the other pieces," said Mrs. Hatch. "I hope the xylophone can be mended and will make some little boy or girl happy."

"Thank you very much," said Nan. "I guess I'd better go now."

The sky was clouding up as Nan started back toward Lakeport. She hoped she would be home before dark, and, perhaps, before the threatened storm.

But the dark, heavy clouds spread over the sky, and when Nan came to a fork in the road, she was barely able to read the signpost. However, she thought she remembered the direction and went pedaling on, the xylophone jingling musically on the basket.

Suddenly Nan realized that she was on the wrong road. She turned her bicycle and started off again. It was growing darker. Presently it began to rain.

"Oh, dear, I must hurry," she thought, "or I'll get soaked."

She was pumping up a little hill when, all at once, the pedals revolved too freely.

"My bike's broken!" exclaimed Nan in dismay. "Now what'll I do?" She was still a long way from the Bobbsey house.

In the distance she saw two moving lights. A small truck was coming toward her. Nan thought of holding up her hand and asking for a ride.

"But Mother says I must never ride with strangers," she remembered. "No, I'll just keep walking."

When the truck reached her, it stopped. The driver leaned out and said:

"Having trouble with your bike, little girl? I'll be glad to give you a ride."

Nan was about to refuse, when she realized

the voice sounded familiar. He was the painter who had rescued her when she was locked in Mrs. White's attic!

"Oh, thank you, yes," she said. "Can you take my bike, too?"

"Sure thing." He jumped out.

Getting a better look at Nan, the man recognized her and laughingly asked if she had been locked in any more attics lately! Then he lifted the bicycle into the back of the truck.

"We may be a little crowded in the front seat," the painter said. "Got another passenger."

"Suppose I get in back," offered the passenger, a young man.

"No, stay where you are," said the painter.

As the three rode into Lakeport, Nan learned that the young man, who was very nice, had missed his train a few miles away. The painter had offered to drive him to the Lakeport station to catch another.

"And how are you getting along with your toy collecting?" the painter asked Nan.

"Oh, very well," she replied. "But right now I'm trying to figure out how to run a show and make some money." She told of Ruthie's plight. "If I do, I hope you'll both come to it."

The young man beside her said he would,

if he were in town. "I don't live here," he told her. "This is the first time I've been back in years. I've been here a week trying to locate something, but I didn't have any luck. Well, here's the station," he said, "and here comes my train."

He thanked the painter, wished Nan luck with her work, and hurried off. In a few minutes Nan was in front of her own house. While the painter was lifting out the bicycle, she said:

"I wonder what that young man was looking for? It sounds like a mystery."

"You're right, it does," the painter agreed. "He said he used to live around here. Father was a ship's captain. I think he said his name's Dawson."

Nan stared at the painter. "Dawson?" she repeated. "Why, he must be Philip Dawson, the man my brother has been looking for! And now he's gone!"

CHAPTER XVII

A DOLL'S TOOTHACHE

THE entire Bobbsey family was startled by Nan's announcement that Captain Dawson's son had been riding with her, and then had vanished.

"Gee," said Bert, "if you'd only found out sooner, Sis! Maybe whoever stole the ship model sold it to Mr. Dawson."

"Oh, I don't think so," Nan answered. "Mr. Dawson said he didn't find what he was looking for. I'm sure he hasn't got the model."

"Then you can still hunt for it, and give him his property if you locate it," Mrs. Bobbsey spoke up.

"Freddie and I couldn't find Matey Foster anywhere," Bert told her. "Joe Norton said he'd heard Matey went away on a ship. I hope he gets back soon."

"I almost hope Philip Dawson won't come

138

back until we find either the model or the paper that was in it," said the twins' mother. "It would be very embarrassing to have to tell him both things are gone. By the way, was Mr. Dawson wearing a Navy uniform, Nan? We might trace him that way."

"No," Nan replied. "But we may see him again soon. He promised to come to our show if he were in town."

"Show?" her mother asked her. "What show?"

Nan told about Ruthie Watson not having money enough for an operation, and how she thought the twins might put on some kind of show to raise the needed amount. Mr. and Mrs. Bobbsey looked at each other.

"What kind of show do you want to give?" Mr. Bobbsey asked. "It would have to be good, or you couldn't charge people to see it."

Since Nan had nothing in mind, the family discussed the subject until Freddie and Flossie's bedtime. Then Mr. Bobbsey said:

"I think my Fat Fairy and my Little Fireman had better get some sleep. Upstairs you go, and I'll tell you a story."

Bert, Nan, and their mother continued to discuss the show. Finally it was decided to put on an exhibit at Uncle Linn's toy shop in ten days.

The surgeon could not see Ruthie for at least two weeks, and in the meantime the twins hoped to raise a lot of money.

"I believe an exhibit of dolls showing the dress and customs of various nations might attract a good many people," said Mrs. Bobbsey.

Dinah, overhearing her, told about a woman who had a large collection of dolls of the South.

"A friend o' mine works dere," she said. "Ebery week she has to dust off those lady an' gentlemen dolls. What a job! I'se sure dat lady what owns 'em would lend 'em to you."

"That's fine, Dinah," said Mrs. Bobbsey. "Nan can go to see her and find out."

Just then there came a loud groan from the kitchen.

"What's that?" asked Mrs. Bobbsey quickly.

"Sam," answered Dinah. "He's got a toothache."

Mrs. Bobbsey, Bert, and Nan went out to the kitchen to see if there was anything they could do for Sam. He was holding one hand over his cheek, which was badly swollen.

"I'se goin' to put a peppermint poultice on my toothache," he told them. "I'll be all right, thank you kindly. Now don't yo' all worry."

But Sam was not all right. He suffered all

night, and in the morning decided he must go
to a dentist. Mr. Bobbsey told him to take the day
off.

Bert and Nan went to the toy shop early to
speak to Uncle Linn about the exhibit. Freddie
and Flossie were too interested in what was going to happen to Sam to leave him. They insisted
upon going along to the dentist.

"Yo' just wait outside here," the colored man
directed them, when they reached the dentist's
office. "Look in th' store windows. I'se goin' in
to th' dentist alone."

While waiting, the twins walked up the street.
They stopped to look at Mr. Hewson's burned
toy shop. Carpenters were busy inside.

"Golly," said Freddie, "they work fast. I'll
bet Mr. Hewson can move back here next week."

"Then we can have our 'zibit' upstairs in the
barn," Flossie remarked gaily. "We have to
have a big one and make lots of money, Freddie."

"That's easy," said her twin. "Oh, look, there's
Sam!"

The children raced down the street to meet
him.

"Is your tooth out? Did it hurt much? What
did he do?" they questioned him.

"It sho' is out!" chuckled Sam. "Dat dentist

nearly pulled me along with my tooth! But he got it out, an' I feels bettah!"

He no longer held his hand to his cheek which, the children could see, was not so swollen as it had been the night before.

Sam told the twins to run along to the toy shop. He was all right and was going to work, too.

"I don't need th' day off now," he said. "I'se all cured!"

Freddie and Flossie found Uncle Linn's toy shop a busy place. The kindly man had given his consent for the exhibit. But in order to make room for it, many toys would have to be mended and sent away during the next week.

Bert had brought Charlie and another friend named John along to work. Grace and Nellie were helping Nan. Flossie and Freddie were given a jar of paste, and told to repair some torn paper dolls and animals.

Near them, on a shelf, they noticed a quaint figurine of an old man. The little wooden statue was rather queer looking. The man's mouth was open, and one cheek was puffed out more than the other.

"Look," said Flossie, giggling. "He has a toothache."

"He sure has," agreed Freddie.

The small twins worked a little longer. Then Freddie said:

"You know what, Flossie? We could make him look better."

"How?"

"By pulling his tooth out," said Freddie. "That made Sam look better."

"That's right," Flossie agreed. "But what could we use?"

"This." Freddie held up a wire hook he had made for some toy-repair job.

"Then let's do it," said Flossie.

She reached up and took down the toy man with the swollen cheek. Freddie inserted the hook in the figure's open mouth and caught hold of one of his teeth.

The hook caught. Freddie pulled. Out came the tooth.

But something else happened, too. The whole face of the figurine suddenly collapsed and broke in several pieces.

"Oh!" Freddie exclaimed. "I didn't know it would do that!"

Uncle Linn, coming up behind the small twins, saw what had happened.

"Whatever were you doing?" he asked, sorry to see the toy ruined. It was a rather unusual one from South America.

"I pulled his tooth because his face was swelled up like Sam's," the little boy answered. "I'm awful sorry."

"The face was supposed to be swelled up like that to make the man look funny," said Uncle Linn. "Never mind. You didn't mean to break it. Bert," he called, "see if you can put the swelling back in Old Pantaloon's face."

Seeing Flossie and Freddie looking very sober, he made up a little rhyme for them.

> *"To have a toothache is no fun.*
> *But if it's pulled, the pain is done.*
> *But I am almost sure I can't*
> *Pull a tooth from an elephant."*

"Oo, wouldn't that be awful?" said Flossie, giggling.

The small twins promised not to get into any more mischief. Uncle Linn left them.

"I don't think we should stay here, Freddie," said Flossie a minute later.

"Why not?"

" 'Cause something always happens."

She suggested they go look for more toys. When Freddie reminded her that Uncle Linn did not want any more until after the exhibit, she said:

"I mean toys for the 'zibit.' Let's go home and ask Dinah where that lady with the South dolls lives. We can go to her house and get them."

Freddie was not interested. He thought they should look for old toy fire engines instead.

"Wouldn't it be swell to have some from Washington's Birthday time?" he suggested.

Flossie laughed. "Freddie, you mean George Washington," she said.

There had been a special celebration in school just before Washington's Birthday. Bert had been in a play. He had held an old-fashioned fire hose, and pretended to put out a fire in George Washington's barn.

"Well, anyway, let's go home," said Freddie, and told Nan they were going back to the house. When they reached it, Mrs. Bobbsey said Dinah was downtown shopping for food.

"You might find her at the bakery," she told Flossie, who wanted to talk to the cook. "By the way, while you're there, you might buy a dozen of those sugar cookies your father likes. Here's some money."

Now Freddie had not planned to bother with Dinah and the Southern dolls, but when he heard about the cookies, he changed his mind, and trotted along with his twin. They waited at the bakery a long time for Dinah, but she did not come. Finally Flossie bought the cookies, and the children left the shop.

"I want one," said Freddie, trying to take the bag.

"Just one. I'll give it to you," said Flossie, afraid her brother would help himself to too many.

She took one for herself and closed the bag. As the twins walked along the street, suddenly a great commotion started up in the tree under which they were passing. It was followed by the quick flight of several birds, then a squeaking sound. The children looked up.

"Flossie!" cried Freddie. "There's a monkey up there!"

CHAPTER XVIII

MONKEY BUSINESS

"THE poor monkey!" exclaimed Flossie. "He looks scared."

"I'll bet he's an organ-grinder's monkey," said Freddie. "Yes, sure he is."

Up to this moment the twins had seen only the animal's face, but now the little creature swung himself out onto another branch. They could see he had on a belt from which a small leather strap dangled.

"Where's the organ-grinder man?" Flossie wondered, looking around.

He was not in sight, and the children could not hear any music. They decided the pet monkey must have run away from his master.

"Let's take him home," Flossie suggested.

The monkey seemed to know what the twins had said. He ran farther up into the tree.

"Try and catch him!" Freddie laughed.

Flossie thought she knew a way to get him down. Opening the bag of cookies, she took one out, broke it in half, and held one piece up in the air.

"Please come down, nice Mr. Monkey," she coaxed.

The little animal dropped to a lower branch, but he would not leave the tree. Finally Freddie tossed the cookie up to him. He nibbled it quickly and chattered his thanks.

"If you want the rest of the cookie, you'll have to come and get it," Flossie called to him.

The monkey remained motionless several seconds, then slowly he backed down the tree trunk. When he was sure the children were not going to harm him, he reached out for the rest of the cookie.

At the same time Freddie took hold of the strap, and told the monkey to sit on his shoulder. The little animal seemed very happy to do this.

"I guess you didn't like it in the tree by yourself," said Flossie. "We'll take you to our house. Oh, Freddie, I hope we can keep him, don't you?"

"Sure. Maybe we could put him in the exhibit." Freddie giggled.

When the twins reached home, they went upstairs at once to show the monkey to their mother.

"My goodness!" she exclaimed. "Where did you find this?"

Flossie and Freddie explained, saying they thought the monkey belonged to an organ-grinder. Mrs. Bobbsey agreed.

"Do you s'pose the monkey had a hat he lost?" said Flossie. "I'll get him another one."

She ran off, and took a little red hat from one of her dolls. The monkey grabbed the hat and set it on his head. The next moment he removed it and went walking around the room holding the hat upside down in front of him. He started to chatter.

Mrs. Bobbsey laughed. "He's asking for pennies," she said.

She got one from her purse, and tossed it into the little hat. At once the monkey took the penny out, opened his mouth, and put the coin in his cheek! Then he started walking again.

"He's a hand-organ monkey all right," said Mrs. Bobbsey. "And very likely the poor man who owns him is looking all over for his pet. An organ without a monkey doesn't bring in many pennies."

"How can we find the man?" said Freddie. Secretly he was hoping the owner would not show up.

"Notify the police," his mother answered. "I'll telephone them. Meanwhile, suppose you take the monkey downstairs and give him a drink of water."

"I'll get it," offered Flossie.

"No, I will!" disputed Freddie.

There was a race between the small twins. Freddie won. He got a bowl of water, which the monkey seemed glad to drink. In the midst of this, Dinah came into the kitchen, her arms full of bundles.

"Lawsy me!" she exclaimed. "Where'd dat creature come from?"

The twins giggled, and Flossie said, "Dinah, we went downtown to find you, and we came home with a monkey!"

Dinah laughed until she shook all over. But when the children told her they hoped to keep the monkey, the cook did not like this so much. She said that she was sure Waggo would not like it either.

Presently Mrs. Bobbsey came downstairs. She had been in touch with the police and learned that an organ-grinder named Giuseppe but called Gus had told the police his monkey had run away.

"Gus wants him back at once," Mrs. Bobbsey said. "I told the police to tell him to come here and get his pet."

The smaller twins were disappointed to learn they could not keep the monkey.

"But poor Gus needs him to collect pennies," said their mother.

"I s'pose so," Freddie admitted.

"I'm going to save up pennies and buy a monkey for myself," decided Flossie.

Gus soon arrived at the Bobbsey home with his organ. He proved to be a kindly old Italian who spoke fairly good English. As soon as he saw the monkey, he cried:

"Ah, Beppo! Beppo! Come to papa!"

With a chatter of joy the monkey nestled in Gus's arms.

"You bad boy to run away from your papa," chided the organ-grinder. "Why you do that?"

The monkey kissed him as if to make up for being naughty, and then showed his master the new red hat Flossie had given him.

"You lose hat, bad boy?" said Gus. "New one ver-ee nice, though. Now we go outside and play for nice people. Beppo do tricks."

Gus played several tunes in the yard, while the monkey did standing somersaults, and swung by his tail from the clothesline, going round and round.

"Oh, isn't he cute?" cried Flossie.

"Beppo dance with you," said Gus. "Take the leetla girl's hand, Beppo."

Flossie was delighted and danced around the yard with the little monkey. Then Gus said he and his pet must go, because they had to earn more pennies.

"We bring-a you present, for you be so kind to Beppo," said Gus, as he and the monkey started off. "Tonight, maybe."

Gus kept his promise. Late that afternoon he came back with the most unusual toy the children had ever seen. It was a tiny man with a hand organ and a monkey. When wound up, the toy man turned the handle of the organ, music played, and the monkey did tricks! The twins laughed and clapped.

"The organ-grinder man looks like you," said Flossie.

Gus grinned. "My brother—he mak-a this— mak-a this look like Giuseppe."

"You—you're going to leave this swell toy here?" Freddie asked in amazement.

"Oh, sure," said Gus.

"But it's not broken," Flossie objected.

"Broken? What you mean?" Gus asked.

"We only take broken toys."

Gus took off his hat and scratched his head. Beppo did the same.

"Beppo, this is ver-ee funny," said Gus. "They only play with broken toys."

Suddenly Freddie and Flossie realized Gus did not know about Uncle Linn's toy shop. The twins had their minds so much on collecting broken toys for it that they had completely forgotten about toys for themselves. They explained this to Gus, and Freddie asked:

"Can we really keep this?"

"Sure, leetla boy," said Gus. "I bring him for you and lettla sister. Be careful you *not* break him."

Flossie and Freddie promised and started playing at once with the toy organ-grinder. Gus and Beppo went off.

"I wish Bert and Nan would come home," said Flossie. "I want to show them how this works."

The older twins were not coming home until after dinner, however. They had been invited to have dinner at Aunt Sallie's house, because a man had brought her a large fish he had caught.

"He might as well have brought me a whale," she complained good-naturedly to the twins. "My goodness, it would take Linn and me till Christmas to eat it. Bert and Nan, you'll have to help us out."

After dinner Bert decided to go to the barn and see if a toy he had glued during the afternoon was dry.

"Come on, Watch," he called to the big black dog who had just had his own dinner in the kitchen. "I'll tie you up now for the night."

The dog trotted outside with him. Suddenly he growled and leaped toward the barn. The door was open, and in the evening glow Bert could see a boy sneaking out.

"Hi, there!" Bert yelled, starting to run.

The boy did not stop. On he ran, Watch getting closer every minute.

"Get him, Watch! Get him!" Bert cried.

The boy was heading for a fence back of the toy shop. If he could reach that, he might jump over before the dog could get him.

But Watch was not going to let that happen. Just as the boy reached the fence, the dog leaped and caught him by the seat of his pants.

"Hold him, Watch! Hold him!" Bert yelled.

CHAPTER XIX

FAMOUS RACERS

THERE was a ripping sound as Bert reached the fence. Watch fell back, a piece of cloth in his teeth. The boy who had run from the garage was gone.

"He got away!" cried Bert in disgust.

Bert swung himself over the fence, but the other fellow was not in sight, and Bert could not hear him running. Was he hiding among the bushes?

"Gosh, where'd he go?" Bert wondered as he looked around. "And who was he?"

Presently Watch ran up to Bert. The dog had not been able to clear the high fence, so he had raced around the corner.

"Here's where that guy came over the fence, Watch," Bert pointed out. "See if you can pick up his trail."

Watch sniffed the ground and ran along a

155

short distance. Then apparently he became confused and gave up the chase.

"Maybe the boy lives around here, Watch," he told the dog. "I'll ask Aunt Sallie."

When Bert went back to the house, he asked her and Uncle Linn if they thought it might have been some boy who lived in the neighborhood. They did not think so and could not imagine who the intruder could have been.

"I can find out from this piece of his pants that Watch got." Bert smiled. "And the first person I'm going to look for is Danny Rugg!"

The piece of cloth was of brown-and-white tweed.

"It'll be easy to find out who owns a pair of pants like this," said Bert to Uncle Linn.

"I'm not so sure of that," said the toy mender. "There must be lots of boys in Lakeport wearing such pants."

Nan giggled. "But now there's one pair of pants that won't be worn at all," she said, "so how are you going to find out, Bert?"

Bert had not thought of this. The piece of cloth was a good-sized one. Nan was right. More than likely the pants would not be used again.

"Do you think the boy took anything from the toy shop?" Nan asked.

"Let's find out," said Bert.

The twins and Uncle Linn hastened out to the barn. So far as they could tell at a glance, everything was in place.

"I couldn't say for sure nothing's been taken, though," said Uncle Linn. "There's certainly a pile of stuff in this place."

"Maybe that boy was only looking around," Nan suggested kindly.

"In that case, I'll bet he *was* Danny Rugg," Bert spoke up. "And I'll bet he was looking for the ship model."

Bert put the piece of cloth in his pocket. He would use it to try finding out if Danny were guilty.

The twins went home. Flossie and Freddie had gone to bed, but Mrs. Bobbsey showed Bert and Nan the attractive little organ-grinder toy which Gus had left.

"This is darling," said Nan, sorry they had missed seeing the real organ-grinder and his monkey. "We'll certainly have to put it in the exhibit. Say, Bert, aren't you going to have some kind of exhibit of your own?"

Bert grinned. "I wanted to surprise you," he said. "But I'll tell you. I'm going to have an exhibition of ship models."

Bert said he had another idea in mind too. This one he could not tell his twin, because actually it was an idea of Freddie's. Freddie had asked Bert to help him and not tell anyone else.

"We're going on a hunt tomorrow morning," said Bert.

The two boys set off together early the next day. Their main objective was ships, but Freddie hoped to pick up something for his exhibit. Uncle Linn had said a Mr. Framm in Reddington, a few miles away, carved and sold models. He might be willing to tell the names of people to whom he had sold some, and perhaps the Bobbseys could borrow them for the exhibit.

"We'll take a bus," said Bert.

Freddie liked this. He insisted upon sitting directly back of the driver, so he could watch him. The little boy never ceased to be amazed how a bus driver could do so many things at once; make change, call out streets, open and close the doors, and guide the big bus safely through traffic.

"I'm going to be a bus driver when I grow up," Freddie announced.

The man heard him and smiled. "Maybe you can take over my job when I'm old," he said.

When the driver called out Lake Street in

Reddington, Bert and Freddie got off and walked to the home of Mr. Framm, the young model maker. The boys were amazed at his workmanship. The place was filled with perfect little ships with tiny hatchways, masts, rigging, and eye-size portholes.

"They're certainly swell," said Bert.

Mr. Framm showed the boys his whittling knives that ranged in size from a carving knife down to the tiniest penknife they had ever seen.

"Don't you ever cut your finger?" Freddie remarked.

Mr. Framm laughed. "I'm sorry to admit it, but every once in a while I do."

"Do you do all your work with these knives?" Bert asked. "Don't you use any machines?"

Mr. Framm said he did not like to use machines. He prided himself that everything he did was handmade.

Suddenly Bert had an idea. "Did you ever know a Captain Dawson?" he asked. "He made ship models, too."

Mr. Framm said he had not known the captain, but that he did know his son Philip.

"Honest?" Bert exclaimed excitedly. "We've been trying to find him; at least, we *were* trying to. Where does he live?"

Unfortunately Mr. Framm did not know. He had met Philip Dawson at an exhibit of ship models in New York. Philip had told him about the captain, and how Philip had been looking in vain for a certain ship his father had carved.

"We had it for a while," announced Freddie. "But somebody stole it!"

"We hope to get it back and give it to Mr. Dawson," said Bert.

Mr. Framm was amazed at the story and promised to tell the captain's son about the Bobbseys if he should meet him again.

Bert now told Mr. Framm about the toy shop, and how they were going to run an exhibit to raise money for lame Ruthie Watson. He asked Mr. Framm to tell him the names of people who might lend outstanding ship models for the exhibit.

"Indeed I will!" Mr. Framm replied.

He got a paper and pencil and jotted down several names and addresses.

"I'll be glad to lend you any of mine which interest you," he said. "Suppose you look around the shop."

Bert did not recognize any of the little ships that stood on the shelves. But when the man explained that one was a model of the *Resolute,* another the *Enterprise,* and a third the *Rainbow,* all famous racing yachts, Bert asked to borrow them.

"I'll come for them the day before our exhibit," Bert told him.

Bert and Freddie left the place feeling that they had made an excellent start. If the people on the list he had given them were as kind as Mr. Framm, the boys would really have a very fine exhibit.

"And we'll make lots of money for Ruthie," Freddie crowed.

At each house where they stopped, the owner of a fine ship model was glad to lend it for the exhibit. By the time Bert and Freddie got back to Uncle Linn's, they were bursting with news. The toy mender was delighted, too. He said he liked no kind of toy better than little ships.

It was too late in the day for Bert and Freddie to do any work in the shop, but before going home they tried to decide where to put the ship models. Freddie wanted them down low where little people like himself could see them. Bert felt they should be up high so visitors would not touch them.

"Maybe we'd better talk to Nan and Flossie," said Bert. "They have to have a good place for their doll exhibit."

"Sure," said Freddie.

Uncle Linn had gone up to the house. Bert followed to ask him how much space they could take for Freddie's surprise. Freddie hung back. He loved the shop, which now was being called the Bobbsey Twins' Toy Shop by everyone.

It was not very light in the place, because there were only two small windows, and the big front doors had been closed except for a narrow space.

Freddie, standing with his back to the stairway to the second floor, suddenly heard a whirling sound. At first he thought it came from outdoors. Then he realized it was inside the toy shop. But he realized it too late.

Something hard hit Freddie Bobbsey from behind!

CHAPTER XX

FLOSSIE'S HUNT

THE force of the blow made Freddie cry out. As he put up his hand, he heard the strange whirring sound again. Before the little boy could move, something hit him a glancing blow on the back of the head.

"Ow!" he wailed, and dived under a bench.

A third object flew past him and landed somewhere with a thud. Freddie waited. When nothing more happened, he peeked out from his hiding place. On the floor near him lay two toy airplanes.

"They're rocket ships!" he said. "Gee, they sure can hit hard." He reached up to feel the back of his head. There was a good-sized goose egg on it. "But who made 'em go?" he asked himself. "Nobody's here!"

For a moment Freddie thought perhaps there was someone else in the toy shop, and he was a little frightened. As he stood wondering what to do, Uncle Linn and Bert came back.

"A rocket ship hit me!" Freddie shouted.

"Oh, goodness me!" said Uncle Linn. "I forgot about the rocket ships! I'm sorry, Freddie. Did they hurt you?"

"My head's bigger'n it ought to be," Freddie complained. But the interest in the rocket ships made him forget the bump. "Where'd you get them, Uncle Linn?" he asked.

The toy mender grinned. "I didn't mean to have my surprise go off when I wasn't looking. Come, I'll show you."

He led the boys to the back of the barn. Though it was fairly dark outside they could see a very fascinating toy airfield standing on a workbench. Uncle Linn said the reason they had not noticed it before was because he had covered it up. The cloth cover apparently had fallen off.

"But what made the rockets go?" Freddie asked.

"Each one has a little gadget like an alarm clock," the toy mender explained. "You set each rocket ship for the time you want it to go off. To tell you the truth, I thought I'd have to work on these some more before they would fly."

"You mean someone sent them in to be mended?" Bert asked him.

Uncle Linn Smith's eyes twinkled. He owned up to having put the little gadget into the toy himself.

"The rocket ships could fly before," he said, "but I thought it would be better if they could start off at different times, one right after the other, so I put in the little alarm clocks."

Bert and Freddie looked at him in amazement. Uncle Linn was not only a toy mender. He was an inventor as well!

"Gee, that's swell!" Bert exclaimed.

"Please show us how they work," said Freddie.

"And give my secret away?" Uncle Linn teased him. "Well, if you promise not to tell anyone, I'll show you the little gadgets I put on the rocket ships."

Both boys were intrigued by the invention. Freddie could not understand it—in fact, it was even a little too complicated for Bert. But both boys enjoyed setting the little markers to ten seconds on one ship, fifteen seconds on another, and twenty on the third, turning the keys, and watching the rocket ships zoom at intervals across the barn.

"Are you going to have this in the exhibit?" Bert asked the toy mender.

"I thought I might."

"Let's charge children a penny to play the game," Bert suggested.

Freddie wanted to know whether one child could have more than one chance. Uncle Linn laughed, and said that would be up to the child.

"Only," he added, "I believe we'll have to play this game outdoors. We wouldn't want to hit anybody on the head, would we, Freddie?"

"I should say not," Freddie answered, and felt of the goose egg on the back of his own head.

Uncle Linn put his hand on the bump, and said:

> *A goose can lay an egg*
> *Bigger than a hen.*
> *When it's on Freddie's head,*
> *He's glad it isn't ten!*

"And now," he continued as the boys chuckled, "I think we'll close up shop for the night."

Watch was tied to the barn door as usual, and was told to guard it very carefully. They wanted no more unwelcome intruders.

The next morning when Freddie looked for

Flossie to go with him to the toy shop he could not find her.

"I saw her go to the kitchen," his mother said.

Freddie went to the kitchen. "Where's Flossie?" he asked Dinah.

"Gone out," was the answer.

"Where?"

"I dunno. She jes took some cookies an' said she was goin' huntin'."

Freddie felt sorry that Flossie had gone hunting without him; it sounded as if his twin might be off on some exciting adventure.

"Where do you think she went, Dinah? To the store?"

"Mebbe. Anyway, she took all her money."

"She did?"

"Yes. She shook up her piggy bank, and took every cent."

It was not often that he and his twin emptied their little savings banks.

"I wish I knew where she went," he said. "Did she take anything else with her?"

"Now let me see," said Dinah. "Seems to me lak she took dat towel I gave her."

"Why did she want a towel?" Freddie asked, perplexed.

"To shake th' money onto from her piggy bank, so's it wouldn't roll off th' table."

"And Flossie took it along? Maybe she tied the pennies in it," Freddie suggested.

"No, she put 'em in her pocket," Dinah told him. "She put th' towel 'round her neck."

Freddie was completely puzzled. So were his mother and the older twins. After a while they became alarmed. Flossie was not at the homes of any of her friends, nor had anyone they asked seen her.

"Oh, dear," said Mrs. Bobbsey. "I can't understand it. Flossie never goes off without telling me where she'll be."

Actually Flossie had not planned to go very far. Susie Larker had told her someone on the next street had a monkey for sale. Ever since Gus and Beppo had been at the house, Flossie had wanted very much to have a monkey for herself.

Susie had not known in which house the monkey lived, so Flossie had gone from home to home asking for him. No one had an animal for sale, so Flossie had to give it up. Disappointed, she had started for her own home, when Sam came along the street in one of the Bobbsey lumber trucks.

"Oh, Sam!" she cried out. "Will you take me on a very 'portant errand?"

Sam thought Flossie's mother had sent her on the errand. He grinned, showing his fine, white teeth, and told her to hop aboard.

"I want to go to West Street," she said. "It's across the railroad tracks."

Sam said, "Yes, I know," and drove to the other side of Lakeport. He wondered what Flossie's errand was, but she did not tell him. Finally, when they reached West Street, she asked him to stop. As she got out of the truck, Sam noticed that the fuel gauge was almost at the empty mark.

"I'll meet yo' here in five minutes," he said. "I'se got t' git this tank filled, or we all will be walkin' home!" He drove off.

Now Flossie had remembered that Gus and Beppo lived on West Street. She had decided to ask the organ-grinder where there was a monkey for sale. A woman, who was weeding her vegetable garden, pointed out his house. Flossie went to it, and rang the bell.

The kindly Italian organ-grinder came to the door. Beppo was perched on his shoulder. The two were just starting out on their day's work.

"Good morning, Gus," said Flossie. "I've come to buy a monkey. I think I have enough money now. Oh, let me hold Beppo!"

At first Gus did not understand. Then he remembered Flossie, and how she had helped him recover Beppo. He thought she had come to buy his pet.

"So sorry! I not sell my Beppo," he said.

"Oh, I don't mean Beppo," Flossie answered quickly. "I mean another monkey. Can you get me one?"

"You want some more toy?" Gus smiled, as Beppo chattered loudly.

"No, a real, live monkey like Beppo."

"Did your mama say you can have monkey?" Gus asked her.

Flossie hung her head. "N—no," she owned up. Then quickly she said, "I'm sure it'll be all right."

Gus shook his head. Flossie must get permission first. His wife came to the door. To make the little girl feel better, she invited her inside and showed her an unusual doll from Italy.

"Oh, may we borrow her for our 'zibit'?" Flossie asked, happy again.

It took some time for her to make Gus and his wife understand about the exhibit. But finally they said they would be very glad to have the doll shown. Flossie said she would come back for it.

"I better go now," she said. "Sam'll be waiting for me."

Sam was not waiting for her, however. She walked up and down the street. Then she went around the corner to look for him, and walked several blocks.

"Oh, dear, where is he?" she said. "I guess I better go back to Gus's house."

But she could not find Gus's house. Suddenly Flossie realized she was lost. Tears rolled down her cheeks.

CHAPTER XXI

FOLLOWING A CLUE

FLOSSIE BOBBSEY remembered that her mother had often said if her children were lost they should stand still and think hard what to do. So now Flossie, fighting back the tears, thought hard.

"I must find a policeman," she said. "He'll take me home."

The little girl wandered up one street and down another. There was no policeman in sight. Then, as she stood wondering what to do next, she looked up. Right in front of her was Gus's house!

Skipping up the front steps she rang the bell. Gus's wife came to the door. She was very much surprised to see the little girl back again.

"Oh, you come for doll?" She smiled. "Or maybe to see monkey? Beppo gone."

"No," said Flossie. "I'm lost. Can you take me home?"

The woman asked where the Bobbsey house

was. When Flossie told her the address, Gus's wife shook her head. She did not know where the street was. But suddenly she had an idea.

"You come with me, leetla girl," she said, taking Flossie's hand. "I find you ride."

Quickly she walked to a house not far away and hurried down the driveway alongside it. In the rear stood a horse and cart. A man was just coming from the house to drive away.

"Nick! You wait!" cried Gus's wife. "Take leetla girl home."

There followed a conversation in Italian. Nick kept bobbing his head. Finally he turned to Flossie and said:

"You climb up. I take you to your mamma."

Flossie climbed to the seat. Nick swung himself aboard and made a clucking sound. The horse started off.

Flossie waved good-bye to the woman and thanked her for her help. Then she said to Nick:

"What do you do with this wagon?"

"Looka for junk. Today is fine day of sunshine. Today I will make lot of money."

Flossie thoroughly enjoyed her ride across town with the junkman. She learned that he stopped at almost every house in town.

"Maybe you know a man my brother is looking for," said Flossie. "His name is Philip Dawson. We have his boat."

Nick did not know Philip Dawson but promised that he would give him the message should he ever come across him.

As Nick and Flossie reached the Bobbsey home, she found an excited group on the front lawn. Among them was Sam.

"Oh, yo's home again, honey chile! Thank goodness!" he exclaimed. "I done thought yo' walked home by yo'self."

Flossie told the whole story of her adventure. She suddenly realized that she had been naughty in not telling anyone what her plans were. Flossie was sorry to have worried everyone, but she told herself that if she had not lost Sam she never would have had the ride in the junk wagon.

The twins did not go to the toy shop until after luncheon. Bert had brought home the xylophone Nan had collected, to fix it. He spent the rest of the morning hammering out two pieces of metal in the Bobbsey cellar. Finally he got them the right size and shape for the F and G notes which were missing.

"But they sound awful," he admitted to Nan, after he put them in place.

His twin giggled as she agreed with him. The metal pieces not only did not sound like the notes F and G; they did not sound like any notes at all!

"Gosh, what am I going to do with this thing?" asked Bert. "We can't give it to anybody this way."

Nan did not think so either. Mrs. Bobbsey was not at home for the children to consult.

"I wonder if Dinah can help us," said Nan. "Let's ask her to come down."

Dinah had a very good singing voice. They found the cook could hold a note for a long time. She offered to sing an F while Bert filed one end of the metal piece.

Nan got to giggling so hard she had to sit down. The picture of fat Dinah, her hands on her hips, her head thrown back and holding a note until the girl thought she would burst, was very comical!

Next to the cook stood Bert filing a little, hitting the metal, filing some more, and hitting it again until he was red in the face!

Nevertheless, the scheme worked. After an

hour the F and G notes were in perfect tune. Dinah, however, was nearly exhausted.

"I ain't blowed an' sung so much since I come to the Bobbsey house," she said, sitting down on a bench and fanning herself.

Nan offered to get lunch so Dinah might rest. But the good-natured woman waved the suggestion aside.

"Just a little singin' spree ain't goin' t' get me down." Dinah laughed. "In five minutes I'll be as good as new. And we's goin' t' have a soufflé fo' lunch, and Nan don't know how t' make dat, I'se afraid."

"You're right," said Nan. "But someday please teach me how to make a soufflé."

"What's a sou—souplay?" asked Freddie Bobbsey, clattering down the stairs to the cellar. "Is that what Dinah was singing?"

The others laughed and told him a soufflé was a fluffy baked dish made with eggs. Unless it was made just right, it would turn out to be one inch high instead of four inches.

"Can you make it six inches high?" Freddie wanted to know.

"I reckon I could," Dinah beamed.

She did manage it, and the Bobbsey twins

thoroughly enjoyed the soufflé, as well as the toast and jam that went with it.

That afternoon when the children reached Uncle Linn's toy shop they learned that a telephone message had come for Nan. A woman who had visited Norway and Sweden had a collection of dolls from those countries. She had heard about the toy-shop exhibit and wanted to lend Nan the dolls.

Nan went to the woman's house. She found the collection to be very fine, and said she would come for it the day before the exhibit.

As she went down the front steps, Nan realized she was not far from Ruthie Watson's home and decided to stop in to see how the lame girl was. When she got there, Ruthie was sitting in a big armchair by the window, holding the beautiful queen doll in her arms.

"Hello, Ruthie," Nan greeted her. "I thought I'd stop in and see how you're getting along."

"Just fine," Ruthie said bravely. "Oh, Nan," she added, "this is the loveliest doll I ever saw. Whenever I get mad at my old crutches, I look at those beautiful blue eyes of hers, and then I feel happy again."

"Ruthie—" Nan began impulsively. She

hadn't meant to tell the little girl about the twins' plans until they were sure they could raise enough money for her operation. But everyone was being so kind and helpful, the exhibit was bound to be a success!

"Ruthie," Nan began again, "you'll be walking without your crutches, and in a little while, too! Pretty soon you'll have all the money you need for the operation, and can go to New York!"

Ruthie gasped in amazement as Nan told her the plan the Bobbseys had. Then she began to ask excited questions about the toy exhibit, and Nan answered them all as well as she could. Finally Ruthie leaned back in the big chair and sighed happily.

"Oh, you're wonderful twins!" she exclaimed. Then she added eagerly, "I want to help, too, Nan. Isn't there something I can do?"

"Of course there is," Nan said kindly. "Lend us your queen doll to put in the exhibit. We could never find another doll as beautiful as she is."

"Oh, I will, Nan, I will!" Ruthie held out the doll impulsively. "Here, Nan, take her right now!"

Nan took the doll, smiled, and rose to go.

"We'll take good care of her until you get her back," she promised.

When Nan reached the toy shop, she found Bert about to start for an electrical store in the business section of Lakeport.

"If you'll wait till I find a safe place for this queen doll, I'll go with you," Nan offered. "I promised Mother I'd go to the bakery near there."

In a few moments she rejoined Bert and the twins started out together. Bert said he had to get batteries for a toy telephone he had brought in. He and Uncle Linn thought they might rig up the telephone between Aunt Sallie's house and the barn. There were many times when Mrs. Pry wanted to speak to her brother, and she always had to come outside when he was in the toy shop.

"But wasn't the toy phone supposed to be given away to some child?" Nan objected.

"Not this one," Bert said, grinning. "This came from Bert Bobbsey."

"Oh," laughed Nan. "Is it the one you and I used to talk over, up and downstairs?"

"That's it," her twin answered. "Do you remember the time I fooled you and said the house was on fire, and you should come right downstairs?"

"Yes, I remember, you old meanie. I grabbed up all my clothes and dolls and everything. Then I had to put them all away again."

"But you got square with me," said Bert, "when you got me downstairs that time you said Danny Rugg was there and was running away with one of my toys. And he wasn't there at all!"

The twins had now reached the store that sold electrical equipment. Nan went off on her own errand, and Bert walked into the store. Inside he saw a familiar figure standing at a counter. And the familiar figure was wearing a coat that instantly made Bert Bobbsey suspicious.

The boy was Danny Rugg, and the coat matched the piece of material which Watch had ripped from someone's pants!

CHAPTER XXII

THE TOY TELEPHONE MESSAGE

DANNY RUGG was wearing plain brown trousers now. But Bert was sure that the pair that matched the coat were the ones that had been ruined by Watch. He marched up to Danny, who was looking at a radio, and said:

"Danny, what were you doing in Uncle Linn's barn last night?"

The boy wheeled around and said, "I was looking for—" Then he stopped short and faced Bert Bobbsey. "What do you mean?"

"You know what I mean," said Bert. "You were told to stay out of our toy shop. You had no right to come sneaking around. You'd better tell me what you were doing there."

"Say, listen, who do you think you are?" the bully snorted. "I'm not sayin' I was in your old barn, but if I wanted to go there I guess I could, and you couldn't stop me!"

The boys had raised their voices. Now several

people in the shop looked at them and one of the clerks called out:

"Pipe down, boys. If you want to fight, go outside!"

"I'm sorry," Bert apologized politely.

Danny Rugg did not apologize. He gave a box on the floor a vicious kick and walked out of the shop.

Bert was disgusted. He was tempted to follow the rude boy and have it out with him, but he concluded the bully probably would admit nothing. So Bert went to the counter and made his purchase of batteries.

By the time he got back to the toy shop, his friend Charlie Mason was there to help him. The boys had planned for several days to rig up the toy telephone under Uncle Linn's direction.

"We'll need a ladder to string the wires across the driveway," Bert told the toy mender.

"There's one in the cellar," said Uncle Linn.

Bert recalled that the express company's truck often came to the barn. The wires would have to be very high for the truck to clear them. After a conference it was concluded to run the wires directly from the second floor of the barn to the second floor of Aunt Sallie's house. Then the wires would be run down the sides of the buildings to ground level.

Uncle Linn's arm was still in a sling, so he could do little toward helping. But he told the boys just where to put everything and how tight to draw the wires.

"You have to have some play in them," he called up a little later, as Bert and Charlie pulled the wires very taut.

"So the birds can swing on them while they sing?" Bert grinned. Of course he knew it was because storms often snap tight wires.

The boys worked over an hour before they had the wires ready. Then the little bell boxes were fastened into place in the barn and the house. Finally the toy telephones were attached at each end.

"Now I believe it will work!" Uncle Linn said. "I'll go to the barn and call you up."

The boys waited several minutes after they thought the toy mender had reached the shop. They had just concluded the telephone was not working yet, when the bell tinkled. Eagerly Bert picked up the instrument. But instead of Uncle Linn's kind, merry voice he heard gruff, startling words:

"Give me that money, Linn Smith! Hand it over quick!"

"What's the matter?" Charlie Mason asked, as a strange look came over Bert's face.

"Th-there's a robber in the barn!" Bert shouted, putting down the toy telephone and racing out the back door.

Charlie was hot on his heels. Panting, the two boys rushed into the toy shop. Too late Bert realized he should have called the police. He and Charlie would have to face the robber alone!

There was no one in sight. Quickly the boys ran up one aisle and down another. They could find no one.

"D—do you suppose the robber took Uncle Linn away?" Charlie quavered.

Just then the toy telephone in the barn rang. Bert grabbed it up.

"Hello! Hello!" he said excitedly.

"Help! Help!" came Uncle Linn's voice from the other end of the wire.

"He's at the house!" Bert shouted. "Come on!"

The boys dashed back to Aunt Sallie's house. But when they reached it, Uncle Linn was not there.

"This is awful!" said Bert.

"What'll we do?" cried Charlie.

Suddenly, as the toy telephone rang again, Bert had an idea. When Charlie jumped to answer it, Bert said:

"Don't pick it up!"

"Why not?" Charlie wanted to know.

"I believe Uncle Linn's playing a joke on us," said Bert. "Come on. We'll find out."

This time the boys went out the front door of Aunt Sallie's house. Skirting the property, they came to the rear of the barn. Bert peeked through a window. Then he laughed.

"Uncle Linn's all right," he said.

"But maybe he was robbed just the same," said Charlie, still excited.

The two boys entered by the rear door. Uncle Linn pretended to look frightened. His bluff worked on Charlie, but Bert said:

"You certainly had us fooled, Uncle Linn."

The toy mender laughed heartily at his little joke until he heard that Bert had thought of calling the police.

"I'd have felt foolish if a policeman had come to the barn," he said.

Bert grinned. "Anyway, if a fellow down here ever does need help, we know he can phone the house."

"Yes, it will be good—*if* Sallie hears the bell."

said Uncle Linn. "Well, we'd better get down to serious business now," he said. "Our exhibit's not many days off."

"When is Mr. Hewson going to move out of the second floor?" Bert asked.

Uncle Linn said that the burned store had been partly rebuilt, and Mr. Hewson would be able to move out of the barn the following day. The second floor was to be used for the ship models; and also for Freddie's surprise airplane models which he had been collecting.

"Gee, there's a lot of work for us," said Bert.

Freddie had insisted that he was in charge of the airplane division. He had worked very hard and had managed to keep out of mischief a long time. Mr. Bobbsey had promised to let Sam drive the little boy around in the truck the day before the exhibit to pick up the small airplanes. When the morning of that important day arrived, poor Sam stood in the kitchen and scratched his head.

"I don't know how I'se goin' t' be three people," he said, but grinned good-naturedly.

"Why do you have to be three people?" Freddie asked him.

"Well, I'se a airplane collector," said Sam.

"An' a ship model collector, an' den I'se got t' be a doll collector, too."

Each of the twins had asked his help for that day, without telling the other children about it.

"I guess yo' daddy will have t' give me th' day off sho' nuff," Sam chuckled.

"I'll ask him," Freddie offered, running upstairs to speak to his father.

Mr. Bobbsey was glad to let Sam help the children. With a twinkle in his eye, he said that he hardly thought the lovely dolls to be collected should ride in a lumber truck, though.

"Mary," he said to the twins' mother, "can't you take the ladies to the exhibit in our upholstered car?"

Mrs. Bobbsey laughed and said she would be glad to. Then, with a twinkle in *her* eye, she told Freddie she hoped no policeman would arrest her.

Freddie looked frightened. "Oh, Mother," he cried, "I don't want you to get arrested."

"Well, you know, dear," his mother said, "our car holds only six people. If I put twenty-five passengers in it, a policeman may stop me, don't you think?"

Freddie knew now that he was being teased.

He was glad, however, that his mother would take care of the dolls. This would leave Sam and the truck for him and Bert.

The ship models were picked up first. To speed up the work, Sam carried several of them from the collectors' homes and helped set them in place around the walls of the second floor in the barn. Then he and Freddie went off to get the airplane models. There were not many of these, so by three o'clock he and Sam had put the last one in the truck.

As Freddie carried the first airplane model up the stairs—he was being extremely careful— Bert called to him to wait a minute. His small brother halted on the top step and looked around. Bert had rearranged some of the ship models and now they covered the entire second-floor shelves.

"Don't bring the airplanes up here yet," said Bert. "We'll have to figure out a place to put them."

"I have it all figured out," said Freddie, marching into the room. "I'm going to hang them from the roof—I mean those beams up there."

Bert looked up. "That's not a bad idea," he conceded. "But who's going to put them up?"

"I am," said Freddie stoutly.

"You?" laughed Bert. "Why, you couldn't reach up there even on the tall ladder."

"Well, Daddy's going to help me," said Freddie. "He told me he'd come here at four o'clock."

In the end both Mr. Bobbsey and Sam were needed to tie cords to the beams and attach them to the airplane models. When all of the models had been hung in place, the Bobbsey group gazed at the second-floor exhibit.

"It sho' looks mighty pretty," Sam commented. "I hopes yo' all has lots of people comin' t' see 'em."

"It's swell," said Bert in admiration. "Look at those little planes up there."

"They're flying," said Freddie excitedly. A draft through the barn made the models sway back and forth.

"No extra charge for seeing the planes in motion." Mr. Bobbsey laughed. "Now we go home to eat."

Directly after supper, Bert started back to Uncle Linn's barn. Watch had hurt his foot and was spending the night in the dog hospital. Because of this, Uncle Linn had asked Bert to come back and stay in the toy shop for half an hour, while the toy mender ate his supper.

Bert went down the street whistling. In spite of the theft of the ship model, he was very happy thinking how well the exhibit at the toy shop looked. He would not have whistled so merrily, if he had known that two figures were following him.

As Bert reached the barn, he found Uncle Linn there with a lantern. He had just come downstairs, after making sure everything was in order.

"Do you think the toy models will be safe here tonight?" Bert asked him.

"Yes." The toy mender smiled. "The place won't be unguarded one minute. Oh, I forgot to tell you," he added, on his way out, "I've asked the police to keep an eye on the shop from nine o'clock on."

Left alone, Bert took the lantern and started for the stairs. Suddenly he heard footsteps behind him. Before he could turn around, someone put a hand across his eyes. As Bert struggled to free himself, two arms grasped him tightly.

"Now don't make no trouble," said a man's rough voice. "I ain't goin' to hurt you. All I want is that paper you found in the model of the *Spray*—and you'd better have it with you!"

CHAPTER XXIII

A CONFESSION

"I HAVEN'T got it," Bert mumbled bravely under the man's hand.

"Then tell us where it is, and the kid here'll get it while I hold you," the man growled.

Suddenly Bert thought of the toy telephone. He was only about a foot from it. He gave a lurch away from the man who was holding him, and kicked the receiver off the hook.

"Help! Help!" he managed to cry before the man caught hold of him again and smothered his yells with a rough hand.

Over at Aunt Sallie's house Uncle Linn heard the little bell tinkle. Picking up the toy telephone, he caught Bert's cry for help and the stranger's gruff words. Alarmed, the toy mender rushed outside and sped for the barn. He was just in time to see a boy running out.

"What were you doing in there?" he called.

Both the boy and the man might have got away

if Aunt Sallie had not come to help, because her brother's arm was still in a sling. She had seen him dash from the house, and suspected something was wrong.

"Danny Rugg!" exclaimed Aunt Sallie, recognizing the boy.

Hearing the voices, the man in the barn dashed out, Bert after him. The fellow tried to run away before Bert saw who he was, but the boy was too quick for him.

"Matey Foster!" he exclaimed.

"Aye, I admit it," said the sailor, seeing that there was no use in running now. "But I wasn't doin' no harm."

"What do you mean?" cried Bert, furious. "You grabbed me and—"

"Now, son," whined the sailor, "I wasn't goin' to hurt you none. I only wanted the note you took out of the ship model of the *Spray.*"

"How did you know there was a note in it?"

"He told me," Matey answered, pointing a finger at Danny Rugg. "I told him I'd give him a dollar toward his new bike if it was true."

Bert glared at Danny. "And how'd *you* find out about the note?"

Danny hung his head. "I heard Flossie and

Freddie talking about it one day at the ice-cream store. And now I want to go home."

"Oh, no, you don't," said Uncle Linn sternly. "You've been entirely too friendly with Matey Foster here. You'd better tell us why."

"Aw, let the kid go," spoke up the sailor. "He ain't done no wrong."

"That's right." Danny brightened.

But they would not release him until he had explained several things. After Danny found out Bert wouldn't sell him the ship model, he decided to annoy him all he could. He had got Matey, who sometimes did odd jobs for Mr. Rugg, to help him. The sailor rented a rowboat for him and he followed Bert to Stony Island. While Bert and Charlie were in swimming, he had taken their boat.

"Did you tell Matey about the ship model?"

"Yes," said Danny. "Right after you wouldn't let me have it."

Danny had spoiled the puzzle the twins had put together, and had come to the toy shop one evening to do more damage, but had been frightened away by Watch. He declared, however, that he had never tried to take the ship model away from the Bobbsey garage.

"You mean you didn't even move it?" Bert asked, amazed.

"No," Danny insisted. "And now please let me go."

"All right," said Uncle Linn, "but hereafter I'd advise you not to meddle in things that don't concern you."

The boy hurried off. Matey Foster tried to go, too, but Uncle Linn would not permit this.

"You've got a lot to explain," he said. "First of all, when did you find out the note was missing out of the model?"

"As soon as I seed the little hatch was open, I—" Matey Foster stopped short. He knew he had said too much.

"So you did steal the ship model!" Bert cried.

Matey shifted from foot to foot. Finally he said, "Aye, I did. But no harm meant. Just curiosity."

"Stealing is more than curiosity," said Uncle Linn sternly. "But if you'll bring the model right back—"

"Oh, belay, I can't!" cried the old sailor suddenly. "I sold it."

He explained that when he failed to find a note in the ship model, he had sold it to a man he had met looking at ships down at the dock.

"I don't know who he was—honest. But I'll try and find him if you'll let me go."

"Suppose you tell us how you got the model in the first place, before you sold it to Mr. Lenter," said Uncle Linn.

Matey Foster confessed he had taken it from the room Captain Dawson shared with his small son when he was in Lakeport. He was angry because the captain had discharged him. In the excitement of the wreck, and little Philip being taken away, no one had noticed the loss of the model. The people who owned the house where they lived had died soon afterward, so Matey felt safe in telling the story that Captain Dawson had given him the little ship.

"So you weren't on the schooner when she went down?" said Uncle Linn. "And all these years you've been saying you were?"

Matey Foster explained sheepishly that he had always wanted to be a hero. No one knew that he had not shipped on the schooner except the crew. So he pretended he had been aboard the vessel.

"And I thought I might get my name in the paper if I gave Philip the model," said Matey. "I'd heard from a fellow in the Navy that Philip was huntin' for it, so—so I was tryin' to get it back, that's all. Danny Rugg told me the model was in Mr. Bobbsey's garage."

Matey Foster declared that he had not been the one who had moved the ship model from the shelf to the front of the Bobbsey garage. Furthermore, he had no idea who might have done so.

"One night my sister Nan was in the garage," said Bert, "and a sailor came there—a tall, thin man. Have you any idea who he was?"

Matey Foster's eyes opened wide. "I thought that was a ghost!" he said. "Belay there, was that your sister?"

Uncle Linn said that a light shining behind a person at a certain height, will throw a tall, thin shadow, even though the person himself may be short and stout. This, then, explained why Nan thought she had seen a tall, thin sailor.

At that moment, footsteps were heard on the driveway, and then a policeman appeared. Matey Foster was turned over to him, and taken away to headquarters. Aunt Sallie declared the affair was now out of their hands.

"And I'm glad, too!" she said. "Well, Bert, you'd better be getting home."

Bert went off. Upon reaching home, he decided to enter the house by the back door. Suddenly he saw a shadowy figure come from the garage. Starting to run, he called out:

"What are you doing there?"

A man began to laugh, and a voice called, "Hello, Bert. Goodness, you sound as if you thought I was a burglar."

"Why—oh, hello, Mr. Dunn," Bert said, recognizing a neighbor of the Bobbseys.

"I just returned two watering cans I took this evening. Your father said I could borrow them any time I wanted to," said Mr. Dunn.

"You—you!" cried Bert. "Oh, gee, one of the mysteries is solved!"

"What mystery?" Mr. Dunn inquired, perplexed.

"You must have moved my ship model," Bert said excitedly. "It was behind the watering cans."

"I sure did," Mr. Dunn replied. "The ship was so pretty, and I was afraid it would fall off the shelf, so I set it on the floor in a corner."

"Oh, wait'll I tell Nan and the others!" Bert exclaimed, dashing off.

His twin met him at the kitchen door. Before he had a chance to speak, she said:

"Oh, Bert! What are we going to do? Philip Dawson is coming here, and we haven't anything to give him!"

CHAPTER XXIV

A GREAT SURPRISE

"WHAT! Philip Dawson's coming here?" cried Bert. "How'd you find out, Nan?"

His twin explained. "Mr. Dawson stopped in Lakeport today on business. He kept meeting people we'd asked about him. So tonight he called up and said he'd come to the exhibit tomorrow."

"Did you tell Mr. Dawson about the ship model and the note?" Bert asked.

"No," Nan replied. "I just said we had something important to tell him. Oh, dear, I wish we could find them before he comes."

By morning, thoughts about the ship model and the note went out of the twins' heads, because there was so much to do for the exhibit. Dinah served them a hearty breakfast, and then they hurried off to the toy shop.

Charlie, John, Nellie, and Grace came to help them. The girls stationed themselves downstairs, so they could explain to the visitors about the dolls of various countries and periods. The boys went upstairs.

"Oh, the queen doll's eyes look so beautiful this morning," Nellie remarked.

"I polished them," said Nan. Then she added, "I think I'll stay near her all day. Maybe somebody can tell me where she came from."

Uncle Linn sat by the door to take in the money from the people who came. They began to arrive early, and in a short time the old barn was filled.

"Why, this exhibit is better than I thought," one man exclaimed as he reached the second floor. "I understand the Bobbsey twins arranged all this."

"How in the world did they ever do it?" said a woman near him. "My husband must see this exhibit."

Everywhere people were voicing their admiration. Most of the men and women who had come left extra money with Uncle Linn. The admission fee was only twenty-five cents, but many people donated an extra dollar, knowing it would go toward an operation for little Ruthie Watson.

"My goodness," said Uncle Linn, when lunchtime came. "Do you know we have nearly enough already?"

The Bobbsey twins were very much excited to hear this.

"I'm going to tell Ruthie Watson," said Nan, "and bring her to the exhibit."

In the rush the children had completely forgotten to invite Ruthie herself. Nan hurried off to the little girl's home. She and her mother were about to sit down to lunch and invited Nan to eat with them.

"Oh, thank you, I will," said Nan. "Ruthie, the exhibit's a big success and the day is only half over."

"Oh, Mother, isn't that wonderful!" Ruthie exclaimed. "I just can't believe it."

Tears of joy came into Mrs. Watson's eyes. After lunch, Nan called a taxicab, and the three went back to the toy shop. Ruthie and her mother were delighted with the exhibit, but the lame girl soon tired, so they did not stay long.

In the meantime Nan had stationed herself again near the doll with the sapphire eyes. Suddenly a woman stopped short and gazed intently at it.

"*Where* did that doll come from?" she asked Nan.

"It was given to the toy shop," the girl replied.

"Don't you realize this doll is a museum piece?" the woman exclaimed. "I'm sure those eyes are genuine sapphires."

"Oh, my goodness," said Nan. "Are you sure?"

The visitor picked up the mysterious doll, examined its clothes, and gazed at its sapphire eyes.

"I'm positive this is the doll that was stolen with some other valuable things from the house of a friend of mine. How did you say you got it?"

Nan told her all she knew. A child had found it on a trash heap on the street and given it to Flossie.

"In Lakeport?" the woman asked.

"Yes," Nan replied.

"I can't understand this," the visitor said. "But I'd advise you to take very good care of the doll. I'll be back later with my friend. She will know if this is her doll."

It was nearly closing time when she returned. With her was a French lady who did not speak English very well.

"Eet eez ze doll," she exclaimed after one look.

The Frenchwoman explained that the doll had been in her family for a long time. When she came to America to live she had brought it with her. She had kept it locked in a suitcase with several other valuable articles. One night, quite recently, her house had been broken into, and the locked suitcase had been one of the things stolen.

Nan Bobbsey supposed that these people were telling the truth, but she was not going to give up the doll until she was sure. Just then her father came into the exhibit and she called him over. When he heard the Frenchwoman's story he remarked:

"Probably the thieves unlocked the bag after they got away. When they saw the doll they didn't realize that it was valuable and so threw it in the nearest ash can. It's a lucky thing they did," he added, smiling.

The Frenchwoman, whose name was Mme. LaFleur, asked Mr. Bobbsey to put the queen doll in a safe place until she could give him proof that the doll was hers. This she could do by showing him a list of all the things she had brought over with her from France, in which was included a description of the doll.

"I am so grateful for eet's return," she exclaimed warmly. "I weel be happy to give ze large reward."

Mr. Bobbsey explained that this was not necessary, but that if Mme. LaFleur wished to contribute to the fund for little Ruthie, the money would be very welcome. Mme. LaFleur promised a generous amount of money, and Nan had only time to say, "That's wonderful," when she spied a young man coming toward her.

"Oh, Daddy!" she cried. "Philip Dawson's here!"

The young man smiled and greeted her with, "This exhibit is amazing!"

"Oh, thank you," said Nan, and introduced him to her father.

"I'm certainly glad to meet you at last," Mr. Bobbsey said, smiling. "My twins have been talking about you for days. You've been known in our house as the mystery man. We all wondered if you would come back."

"We would have had your father's ship model for you, Mr. Dawson, if you'd only come back a little sooner," Bert said regretfully.

"It wasn't Bert's fault," Freddie spoke up stoutly. "Matey Foster took it away from me and then he sold it to somebody, and now it's gone."

Captain Dawson's son began to look very bewildered, so Mr. Bobbsey explained about the theft. When he had finished, Philip Dawson said:

"The whole thing is really a mystery to me, too. My father always told me he wanted me to have the ship model of the *Spray*. I couldn't understand what had happened to it after he was lost. But I was only a kid and they sent me way out West to some relatives, so I couldn't look for it."

Philip Dawson went on to tell them it was not until years later that he had heard his father was supposed to have had money which he had always refused to put in a bank. In the meantime, Philip had joined the Navy and had not had a chance to come back to Lakeport until recently.

There was no more time to hear the rest of his story, as many people were coming in to the exhibit. In fact, the exhibit had become so popular, it had been decided to run it for a few days.

"Mr. Dawson, how about having dinner with us and telling us the rest of your story then?" suggested Mr. Bobbsey. "And we have something else to tell you; something surprising."

"I'd like to come very much," the young man replied.

A few minutes later he drove off with the

twins and their father. When they reached the house, Bert and Nan hopped out with their guest and went up to the front door. Before Mr. Bobbsey could get out his key, Dinah, in a fresh, white uniform and apron, opened the door.

"Oh, Nan! Oh, Bert!" she cried out. "I thought yo' all were never comin' home. Dat paper what got lost out of th' little ship—the one Waggo took away—I believe I done found it!"

CHAPTER XXV

THE UNDERWATER SEARCH

EXCITED questions were asked so fast that poor Dinah could not answer all of them. Instead, she led Philip Dawson, Nan, and Bert into the living room of the Bobbsey home and pointed to Mr. Bobbsey's favorite armchair.

"Dere's where Waggo hid dat paper," said the cook.

"You mean down the side of the chair cushion?"

"That's exactly what I mean," said Dinah. "While yo' all was away this afternoon I caught Waggo diggin' away in dat chair."

Dinah had scolded the mischievous fox terrier, but the little dog had refused to jump down. Finally she had turned back the chair cushion. Immediately, Waggo had pounced on the folded paper that had lain beneath.

"'Course I took it away from him," said Dinah. "Here it is," and she handed it to Bert.

By this time the rest of the family had come in and were as excited as the others at Dinah's find.

"That's the note," cried Flossie. "That's it! Waggo tried to bury the letter like a bone, and then got it out again!"

Bert handed the note to Philip Dawson. The young man's hands trembled ever so slightly as he unfolded the old letter.

"This is from my father all right," he said, "and it's addressed to me."

He read the message slowly, for it was a bit faded. The Bobbseys stood by quietly and waited for him to finish. Finally he said:

"My father hid all his money in the *Spray*. He drew a diagram, showing just where it is; beyond a forward bulkhead of the schooner. The money is in a secret locker in a copper box," Captain Dawson's son went on. "That is, if someone hasn't taken the money, or if the box hasn't sunk out of sight."

"I sure hope it hasn't," said Bert. "Anyway, Charlie and I know where the wreck is."

"That's fine. Then if you'll show me where it is," Philip Dawson said, "I'll get a diver to go down and investigate. There's a diagram here, so it shouldn't be hard for him to locate the box."

"I want to go and watch," Freddie spoke up.

"I'd like the whole Bobbsey family to come with me," Philip Dawson invited.

"Thank you, we'd like to," said Mrs. Bobbsey.

The young man showed them his father's sketch of the forward bulkhead, with measurements, showing just where the secret locker had been located.

"I hope there's a lot of money in it," said Freddie, who could hardly wait for the big day to come.

The next day a truck arrived at a Lakeport dock, with a diver, his outfit, and two helpers. The diver was a pleasant-faced, blue-eyed man named Tom Haley. Philip Dawson introduced him to the Bobbseys, who had gathered for the treasure hunt.

The diving apparatus was transferred to a barge. Then the Bobbseys and the others rowed to the spot where the *Spray* had gone down.

"It's so near Stony Island," said Mrs. Bobbsey, "I can't see why none of those aboard were saved."

"I've been told," Philip Dawson explained, "that there was an explosion on the schooner. The wreck was not caused by the storm."

"All ready!" called the diver. "Help me with my suit, boys."

Tom Haley's heavy rubber suit had been laid out on a bench near a pump. The pump would force fresh air through a rubber hose into the diver's helmet. As he dressed, the diver looked again at the diagram which Philip Dawson was holding.

"This looks easy to find," Tom Haley said.

"Hurrah, I'm going to see a treasure!" cried Freddie suddenly, jumping up and down.

The diver shook his head as his helpers pulled the heavy rubber suit on him.

"You never can tell," he said. "Wrecks are queer things. But if the treasure's down there, I'll find it!"

Lead weights were now fastened onto the back and chest of the diver to keep him from floating to the surface.

"I wouldn't like to be a diver," Nan said with a little shiver.

"I would," declared Freddie. "When I grow up, I'm going to be a diver." Then he laughed. "Mr. Haley looks like a turtle."

It was true. As the diver stood on the deck, his head stuck out of the copper ring of the collar like a turtle's head poking out of its shell.

To the heavy belt of his suit were now hung a crowbar, an ax, and other tools for working under water. The sleeves of the diving suit ended in heavy rubber cuffs around Haley's wrists. He wore no gloves.

"I need my hands free," he told the children.

In his helmet was a telephone, over which he could talk to his assistant on the barge, and to his belt was attached a strong cable.

"That's to send up the treasure box when I find it," he said, smiling.

"Here's hoping," said Philip Dawson. "Good luck!"

"Thanks."

The heavy helmet, with its big glass eyes, one on each side and another in front, was now made fast to the copper collar. Then the diver climbed down a ladder on the side of the barge and disappeared under water.

The men at the pumps turned the handles steadily. Bubbles of air came from the diver's helmet to the surface of the river.

"All right, Tom?" asked the man at the deck telephone. Then in a moment he reported to the Bobbseys and Philip Dawson, "He's almost at the wreck now."

"How long will it take him to get the box out?" asked Bert.

"Maybe an hour," was the answer. "It's pretty hard work breaking through steel."

There was tense excitement aboard the barge, as they all waited. Would the diver find the treasure that had been under water so long?

"Tom says he's hacking away at the bulkhead now," said the telephone operator presently. There was another period of waiting. Then he shouted, "He has the locker open now!"

"Is the treasure in it?" cried Freddie.

There was a pause. The man at the telephone listened, then grinned.

"Yes. It's there!" he shouted. "Tom's breaking it out! He'll send it up as soon as he can!"

Bert and Freddie shouted their delight. Philip Dawson's face was tense in anticipation.

"He's making it fast now," the telephone operator reported. A moment later he called to his helpers, "Hoist away!"

Hand over hand the line was pulled up. In a few seconds a green-colored metal box, about eighteen inches square, broke the surface of the water and was hauled aboard. It dropped with a thud on the deck.

"The treasure!" shrieked Freddie. "Oh, please hurry up and open it, Mr. Dawson."

"Freddie, not so loud," his mother whispered.

She could see that there were tears in Philip Dawson's eyes, as he thought of his father and the life's savings he had left his son. But a moment later the young man smiled at the Bobbseys and said he would open the box at once, so that they might enjoy the surprise with him.

"That is, as soon as Tom Haley comes up," he added. "He mustn't miss this."

The diver was soon on deck. As his suit was being removed, Philip Dawson thanked him and then asked for a chisel and a hammer.

"Guess you'll need them to open that box," said the diver. "I'll help you."

The Bobbsey twins hardly breathed. Then, as the lid was raised, they all said:

"Oh!"

Within the watertight box were bundles and bundles of money. There were also unset precious stones as well as a lot of jewelry. No doubt Captain Dawson had collected the fine gems on voyages to foreign ports.

"It really is a treasure," said Philip Dawson soberly. "And I'm going to share the money with several people I know who need it. Ruthie Watson can have a fine long rest after her operation."

On the way back to the dock, the young man declared he ought to leave Lakeport and get back to his work. Freddie, looking at him, said:

"Please don't go yet. You never saw my airplane exhibit. And it's—it's swell!"

"Well, I couldn't miss that." Philip Dawson
smiled. "Or the ship models either."

Mr. Bobbsey drove them all direct to the toy
shop, and they went upstairs.

"This is a wonderful exhibit," Philip Dawson
said. "As good as any—"

He stopped speaking because Freddie had
suddenly cried out excitedly. Pointing a shaking
finger at one of the ship models in the collection,
the little boy screamed:

"Bert, do you see what I see?"

Bert followed his brother's pointing finger.
The others did, too. There on the shelf, behind
one of the other models, stood the *Spray!*

"*How* did it get there?" Nan gasped.

When the Bobbseys and Philip Dawson had
recovered from their astonishment, they figured
out that the stranger to whom Matey had sold
the model must have been one of the men who
had loaned his collection of ships for the exhibit.

"Sam must have got the *Spray* and set it up
here," Bert said, "and we never noticed it."

Philip Dawson was delighted to have the
ship model at last, but said he was going to let
Bert keep it a while.

"Until I get you another one," he promised.

That evening the Bobbsey twins helped Uncle Linn close the doors of his now famous barn. It had done a worthy job. Starting as a little toy-mending shop, it had grown into a flourishing business!

With the help of the Bobbsey twins, hundreds of toys had been mended and shipped to children who otherwise would have had none. A successful exhibit had been held, and more than enough money had been made to send Ruthie to New York for the operation that would enable her to walk again like other girls.

"This is the most excitingest day I've ever had," said Flossie, as the twins were on their way home.

But other exciting days were to come to her and her brothers and sister. They happened in "The Bobbsey Twins in Tulip Land."

"Everything's fixed up," said Nan, beaming. "Ruthie's going to take the Eskimo dolls and the good-luck coin in place of the queen doll. And did you notice Uncle Linn had his arm out of the sling? Now he can use both hands."

"But it was so much fun I hope he'll still let us help him in the toy shop," said Bert.

All the Bobbsey twins hoped so too!

RC/12